THE ROAD TO RECKONING

Robert Lautner was born in Middlesex in 1970. Before becoming a writer he owned his own comic-book store, worked as a wine merchant, photographic consultant and recruitment consultant. He now lives on the Pembrokeshire coast in a wooden cabin with his wife and children.

THE
ROAD TO
RECKONING

ROBERT LAUTNER

THE BOROUGH PRESS

The Borough Press
An imprint of HarperCollins*Publishers*
1 London Bridge Street
London SE1 9GF

www.harpercollins.co.uk

This paperback edition 2015
1

First published by HarperCollins*Publishers* 2014

Map © David Rumsey Collection
www.davidrumsey.com

Robert Lautner asserts the moral right to
be identified as the author of this work

A catalogue record for this book
is available from the British Library

ISBN: 978-0-00-751130-3

This novel is entirely a work of fiction.
Some characters (or names) and incidents portrayed in it, while based
on real historical figures, are the work of the author's imagination

Set in Minion by Palimpsest Book Production Ltd,
Falkirk, Stirlingshire

Printed and bound in Great Britain by
Clays Ltd, St Ives plc

MIX
Paper from
responsible sources
FSC C007454

Find out more about HarperCollins and the environment at
www.harpercollins.co.uk/green

For my brother

The Lord made men.
But Sam Colt made them equal.

—*Anon.*

ONE

When I first met Henry Stands I imagined he was a man of few friends. When I last knew of him I was sure he had even fewer.

But, it could be said, just as true, that he had fewer enemies because of it.

And as I get older I can see the wisdom of that.

I was twelve when my life began, mistaken in the belief that it had ended when the pock claimed my mother. She had survived the great fire of New York in '35 that we all thought might have quelled the pock.

The pock knew better.

In 1837 my father was a quiet man in a noisy world. At twelve I was not sure if he had been a quiet man before my mother had gone. I can remember all my wooden-wheeled toys, the tiny things for tiny hands that I cherished, but not the temperament of my father before the Lord took Jane Walker. The quietness is more important than that he was a salesman for spectacles, still quite widely known as 'spectaculars' by some of the silver-haired ladies we called upon.

Half the time as a salesman he would just be leaving his card with the maid and the other half would be following up on the business that the card had brought.

That was his day and for some of the week it would be mine also.

It was a slow business and an honest one. Slow for a boy. The closest it ever got to an element of shrewdness was when my father would tell me beforehand to sip slow the glass of milk or lemonade that I was always offered. Sip slow in order to postpone the moment when the lady of the house would be confident in her judgment that she could not afford a new pair of spectaculars today and politely asked my father to leave.

I did not mind to drink slow so much when it was milk or, worse, buttermilk, but the lemonade was hard to draw slow when I had been walking all day. And today if a lemonade comes my way when it is offered I still sip it like it is poison when all I want to do is swim in it.

All of that was in the city of New York, where I was born, and I had no notion of what the rest of the country was like. I also had little idea of what other children were like, being homeschooled by my aunt on my mother's side and mostly staring out our parlor window at other boys pinwheeling down the street.

I was intimidated by their screams and backed away

from the panes as people do now from tigers in the zoological. We had no zoological then but no want of beasts.

I now know this sound of children to have been their unfettered laughter, having had boys of my own once. At the time I thought they were savages, as dangerous as the Indians I imagined hid out on the edges of the roads waiting to snatch me if I did not keep an eye out for them and a piece of chalk to mark behind me, which every boy knew they could not cross.

I am pretty sure it was April when my father had his idea. I remember the crisp blue sky and I know I was still only a part of the way through my Christmas books that I was allowed to read for pleasure on Fridays, and so those weeks would pan out to make it April.

One of them books was about a boy on a ship in the wars against Napoleon, for it rubs at my memory, and the other was set hundreds of years in the future, when the world would be better. I liked that one. It was written by a woman, I remember that, and I imagined that my mother would have liked it. It had a utopian view of our country and my mother was always looking for the best in everything.

I am sorry that I can remember little more about them books but my memory of that time is clouded when it comes to the pleasing and too much of it burned black onto me with the other.

My father had gotten word of a new invention, the chance of a new venture that needed no capital, and I had never seen him so animated. I did not know, as a child, that the whole land was in depression and in New

York in particular businesses and people's homes were crumbling under the weight of paper. I had seen protesters in the park, the placards, and heard the cry. The same as it ever is.

When I think back it would seem that in just a few years, what with the pock and the fire, the banks closing and the gangs, that New York had gone to the Devil. But I was a boy and my belly was full and my aunt had reminded me that there had been some insurance on my mother's life that would see me well but for the fact that I was drawing into it every time I scraped too much butter, which was her curse of me.

I suppose we were also caught in this financial bust, which would cause my father to take to the road, and I also presume that as a businessman my father paid attention to patents and newspapers. But he shared none of this with me. What I have to tell you now is that in April 1837 we traveled to Paterson, New Jersey, in our gig, my father almost jumping all the way and my books and my aunt Mary left behind.

My aunt was not happy about my going on the road, although I regularly traveled with my father around New York, probably more as a sympathy for his sales than for my companionship, which was mute at best, but I gathered from their talk that we would not come home for supper this time.

'You cannot take him, John!' She said this as a fact rather than a plea for my safety. 'You'll be gone for months! And what for his schooling?' This was a good reason for me to run. My aunt had wishes to end my homeschooling. She had subscribed to the *Common School Assistant*, and along with the *Christian Spectator*

4

and *Cobb's Explanatory Arithmetick* this had become her higher learning.

She had become enamored of a new model of teaching from Europe. A studious Swiss named Fellenberg had developed an institutional method that mingled poor and wealthy children. His concept being that the poor in society would be taught the trades and education needed for their place, and the rich would be taught the arts, literature, and politics of their standing. By seeing the poor at their work the rich children would appreciate their contribution to the country, and by observing their betters side by side and seeing them learn how to be leaders and intellectuals the poor would understand the way of things and appreciate that their aspirations were taken care of. I figured I was for the better half of the school and if that mister Fellenberg thought poor children were apt to admire their betters he had never seen the Bowery, and I for one would have none of that.

'What is a boy to do out in the west?' she insisted.

This statement was lost on me. Even at twelve I knew that I would have no limit of things to do out beyond the mountains. My own thoughts of danger were less important than having the opportunity to be away from my aunt's lavender chiffon and her yardstick rule, which I never saw measure anything except how much blame my knuckles could take. Besides, we were talking only as far as Illinois and Indiana in those days. I am sure my father had no intention of entering the wilds of Missouri.

'Tom is coming,' my father said. 'I cannot leave him here. I will need him.'

Against tradition I was not named for my father. We were a book-reading family and he had named me after the Tom in a Washington Irving tale published the year before I was born. It had the Devil in it.

He looked on me with the same strained face that I had awoken to on that winter morning when my mother passed.

He had sat at the end of my bed that dawn, wringing his hands, rocking like a just and sober man down to his last coin with the landlord at the door and plucking at his fingers to count where he had gone wrong.

'I cannot.' He gave the look to me but spoke to my aunt. 'I will not leave him.'

He packed us on that little four-seat Brewster bought from Broad street the year before the fire, in the months when my mother began to look better.

No room for books or toys. And I never noticed that I left these things. My heart was already on the road.

TWO

Our house was near the river in Manhattan and we took a ferry from Pier 18 to Jersey. Jude Brown stomped and complained on the boat all the way and I had to wrap my arm around his neck to comfort him. There in Paterson, New Jersey, my father met with a young man in a black ulster coat and striped trousers and with a fine mustache that he must have been working on hard to remove his youth. He looked and spoke like a sailor and by that I mean he was short but strong and cussed casually when it seemed unnatural to do so in company you hardly knew.

My father was impressed with him instantly. This young man had convinced some New York investors who still had capital to part with their money to fund a firearms company set up in a corner of a silk-works, and there was no doubt in the man that the military would take up his design. It was an absolute certainty. His assurance to us.

My father shook his hand like he was pumping water.

I am sure that this smiling young man had no trouble extracting money from those cigar smokers with their handlebar mustaches and silk coats that they had trouble buttoning up. At twenty-two years or thereabouts he had certainly beguiled my father, a man twice his senior. I would later find that just a few years before he was taking laughing gas around county fairs from a wagon colored like a circus tent and for a half-dime turning the hayseeds into even bigger fools. I suspect he may have had this gas pumped into the factory, so deliriously enthused was my father, and even I myself, who was most suspicious of any person who did not have a key to my house, followed him around the factory like a puppy.

My father willingly signed on for a job for which he would not be paid. Another five minutes and my father would have been paying him. We were being let in on the ground floor of a great enterprise. I noted when we left that there was another gentleman who was also waiting to be let in on this secret ground floor.

It was commission work and I will accept that that is still work, for my father earned the same for the spectacles he sold, but he still had a stipend for his day-to-day living. But people needed spectacles as they were. They did not require reinventing. At the time, beyond his charming of us both, I saw no prospect in this mister Colt reinventing the pistol.

He called it the 'Improved Revolving Gun,' *improved* being normal devious bluffen brag for a stolen idea and snake oil sold from a buckboard.

This young man, Samuel Colt, now famous throughout the world for 'improving' the act of murder, was aware as any that Collier's revolving flintlock was a fine gentleman's gun and that the percussion cap had led to the development of the new Allen pepperbox pistol, which put several shots in a man's fist, mostly the shaky hands of gamblers and barkeeps and others of ill repute whose reputations mister Colt wished to expand by his own invention.

His ambition was to bring unto the world a gun that could be machine made by a labor-line rather than a craftsman. A factory gun. A cheaper gun. The parts could be interchangeable, fixed on the fly (which, in my opinion, was admitting to its faults), and, with a good-sized factory, his arms could be mass-produced for the military.

He had made several hundred revolving carbines and pistols and had provisionally sold some of these down in Texas to the independents (they were fighting with the Seminoles again and always with the Mexicans) and mister Colt claimed that he had won the U.S. patent for his revolving gun the day after the battle for the Alamo began, although he had applied a year before, and, as he declared, if only providence had come sooner the outcome may have been different. He assured my father that he was to be one of the few who would change the course of the history of warfare.

I, to this day, hold to only one truth: if a man chooses to carry a gun he will get shot.

My father agreed to carry twelve.

Mister Colt held his faith in an army and navy contract, be it American, French, or British, for he had traveled and patented the gun to them all, but like any good salesman who is confident in his product, rather than one that sells and runs, he believed that if he put the guns in enough American hands that would do just as well. He kept back in his history that the army had already rejected his weapon as too flimsy for any good field let alone a bad one. It could be disassembled; it could break just as well because of that. Besides, the country was at peace. Even war-makers draw a line at spending sometimes.

So my father was to become a salesman—more, a spokesperson as mister Colt put it—for the Patent Arms Manufacturing Company. We would travel west and promote the gun, the pistol not the carbine, my father well aware that this was not a new thing. Even in New York revolving rifles were sold, although mister Colt was adamant to point out that those were hand-turned and not mechanical and thus just inferior sporting guns. My father took four models each of the machined pistol, all blued steel.

There were four of the belt models with straight, plain grips. Belt model being as imagined: a gun for a man's belt for short duty, for street-work; not noble like a horse-pistol fired from a saddle holster in defense of Indian attack.

Four others were the scabbard type, with longer barrels and larger bore for carrying in leather. These had straight or flared walnut grips like the handle of a plow. The remainder were boxed models of both with tools and fancy linings. Mister Colt declined to offer us to sell the smaller pocket model. He would do that himself from his office in the city. Country-folk, he said, would not need such a small gun.

These were all 'small' guns to my mind when most used musket-bores. And why would someone hinder and confuse himself by carrying two loads of shot, one for his rifle and another for a pistol? That still does not make sense to me. However, mister Colt, a natural carpenter, and by that I mean one of those who can look at trees and envision chairs, had made a wooden model of the gun, which he gave up to me and until that point in my life was the nicest thing I had ever seen made.

This wooden gun replicated the others. That is to say the pulling back of the wooden hammer 'revolved' the wooden chambers of the pistol, and the cylinder locked as on a ship's capstan as it cranked and ratcheted the hawser-chain by the sweat of men. It was on a ship, as he evoked to us both, where mister Colt fancifully dreamed up his design by watching the capstan's ratchets. He had carved this very gun from an old ship's block in the same manner as he had his first. I did not swallow that either.

As the hammer locked, the trigger would drop out from the wooden frame cute as a wooden toy-horse nods as you roll it across the floor, and I, as a boy, thought that he would do a far better trade selling these masterpieces as playthings.

He smiled and put it into my hand and my fist wrapped around the bell-like walnut grip, flared like some of the others, and my body took to it as naturally and as comfortable as shaking a hand. It was a stained dark wood the color of leather. I can see it still, now as I write, and in my mind I become small again, my hand shrunk by the gun. I can smell the oil on my fingers.

Mister Colt patted my head; I was small for my age and men tended to do this. I did not know if they did it to their own. I have never done it.

'Well, Thomas,' he asked, 'what do you think of my gun?'

'It has real beauty about it, sir.' I declared this about the wooden one that I now thought was gifted to me. I would come to despise the iron ones.

If all wars were fought with wooden guns I would not have read a telegram (and mister Colt also had some invention in that bearer of bad news) that told me to dig two graves for my sons when America stopped being his brother's keeper and mowed him down.

I have no doubt that the repeating weapon shortened wars, but only because it multiplied man's ability to shorten the number of his enemies, and not because it would belay the horror of his work.

I was not to have the wooden gun. Its purpose was to enable my father to enter a general store without terror to the owner and demonstrate the practicality of the Paterson, as the gun was named, before securing a sale.

And that was our journey.

My father would gather only orders, take no money, and upon returning to New Jersey, Colt would pay him commission on those orders, mister Colt having informed him that we would be rich in a month. The working samples were to be demonstrated and sold to fund our passage as need may arise; deducted from the commission, naturally.

He never once asked my father, who sold spectacles

to old ladies, if he could load and fire a gun. Hands were shook.

We bought half a wheel of cheese and dodgers and crackers and with only my mother's Dutch oven, jerky, a brick of bohea tea, and a bag of sofkee, for which we would just need to add water to feed an army, it being but little more than cornstarch and rice with some added pease, we set off on what we thought was the best road.

My father told me we had a little over twenty-nine dollars. This was more money than I had ever known in my life and I estimated my father to be a rich man. And this was coin; none of this trust in paper that we have now. I was sure that if I lodged carefully and lived on eggs and candy I could subsist on twenty-nine dollars for the rest of my life.

I was twelve and about to spend more time alone with my father than I had ever done even if you added together all the months of my life.

I will say with excitement even now that the prospect of the road held no adventure greater than the thought of being arm to arm with my father on the seat of our Brewster wagon. Every word he spoke would be to me.

It is a fault of nature that fathers do not realize that when the son is young the father is like Jesus to him, and like with Our Lord, the time of his ministry when they crave his word is short and fleeting.

But for now I had him and we went together and alone. I talked like a bird waking and my father listened all the ways out of New Jersey.

We did not make the west.

THREE

Our gelding, Jude Brown, named on account of his brown eyes and not his fawn-and-roan coat, was a hay horse. This made him slow to the road and, once he got a flavor of the grain we had brought with us, became slower still and fair plodded along as if he carried a whole town behind.

Towns were not those so incorporated that we know now. Boroughs for the most. Some of their names have changed, either through disease or shame, and only their counties remain as their forebears.

We were to travel through Pennsylvania using the lakes, rivers, and canals as our guide, which are the most populous routes, aided with only a compass. This was not such a daunting prospect as it sounds. The method was to visit one settlement and, if successful or not, get

14

directions to the next. A man who does not want to buy your goods is most willing to direct you well to elsewhere. These directions were west anyhow and the road straight.

We camped for the most to save money and I woke almost every day smelling of smoke but glad for it, for April is not a bad month.

Sleeping on the Brewster for fear of snakes and such, I even found comfort in my father's snoring. That was the first time I had ever slept with anybody, having no siblings, and I still do not know why people complain so. I could barely sleep for grinning.

We had flint, striker, and char cloth for the fire and it was my role to gather the wood and stones, which takes longer than you think. The small animals have no fear of you but rather chatter and chide with the birds that you are disturbing their house. We had some anthracite to fire the oven with kindling added and we made our tea first, with water from the rivers, which tasted of iron. We poured out and kept the tea in a kettle and fetched more water for the sofkee and put in the jerky to soften so it became like bacon. With the corn bread on the side, that was our dinner, and we kept to the hours of between noon and three if we were able and ate supper when we felt we had done enough. Supper would be the cheese and crackers and any sofkee meal we had left. At breakfast we would mash the dodgers with water and the scrapings of the sofkee and rewarm our tea, which would make me giddy with its strength overnight.

I did not complain, but I missed eggs and pork and I did not think it would have weighed Jude Brown too much to have carried eggs at least. I think my father had expected more farms or the towns to be larger but he never said a word on this.

Five days in, over the Delaware by ferry, and we had gained a hundred miles and made Berwick before noon. The place was busy with engineers and carpenters, the town having lost its bridge two years before due to an ice flood and keen to have it rebuilt. This progress of the bridge across the Susquehanna had brought great trade, although the men worked for half of what they would have done last year and someone with a big hat and cigar knew that and profited.

A poor businessman will pay his worker as much as he can afford. A rich one, in times disadvantageous, as little as he has to. That is the world. Still is. Your vote will not change it. You know that now. I work my land for somebody else and get on with it beside you. Maybe I am writing this to be a boy again. Maybe you are reading it for the same. A time before writs and accounts. I say a bill is not a bill until they come tapping at your window.

This place, Berwick, at least had hotels, the cheapest being eighty coronet cents and the greatest two dollars. We stayed at the cheapest, which gave us a hammock, but breakfasted farther up the street where we could get ham and eggs for one shilling, our New York term for the Spanish real, but we settled wiser on fried eggs and bread for nine red cents, thinking less of Gould's saloon, where our hammocks were, who would charge you an extra three cents for toast. Even I knew that was costly. Jude Brown ate at the hostler and probably did the better for it.

16

We had made good sales so far. My father sold the Patersons for ten coin dollars, fifteen if it was sold with its kit, which included a spare cylinder and combination tool. That breakfast we had paper orders for one hundred and twenty dollars and even I knew that was not bad. It was with high hearts that we left Berwick, and even Jude Brown could sense our lack of troubles for he fair skipped along. But the towns got smaller, the road meaner, and it is along that a bit that I would meet Henry Stands. We still had the twelve Patersons, the wooden one occasionally my plaything, and I pointed it and shot at ghosts of Indians along the road.

It was the last time I played until I met my own children.

FOUR

We now approached the endless green of the Allegheny mountains, the low end of the Appalachians, which got no closer as you went toward, and we came into the skirts of Milton, still following the Susquehanna. This was a tannery place and also a great lumber town and the air was thick with the smell of sawed wood and the dust of it in your nose. They had a proper sawmill fed by the river and also their own steam-powered mill, which we did not see but did hear aplenty.

It was at that time a bustling settlement where anyone could make a house and call it a hotel. There were tents outside the town and these were the abodes of those waiting for better fortune.

With so much wood there were stores nailed up every day. It had a bank, which was still open, and a main street called Front street although I did not see a Back street to accompany it. Lumber and shingles seemed to be in everybody's hand. This was good to see. Everywhere else the hammers and the pickaxes had gone down. For ten years America had gone through a juncture of construction that had shamed the pyramids. The canals, the roads, and the bridges. Work in one place one day, walk a ways up the road and sign on as a teamster somewhere else. Now the only things building new were prisons. And we were worldwide proud of those.

This is where I will demonstrate how my father worked for Colt and his oddment of a gun, for up until this place we had gone without incident and I am sure that you would find little interest in the ordinary successes and failures of the traveling merchant.

In those days general stores would often have a table or two and double for butchers and feed stores also. Cards and gin probably more their bread and butter than bread and butter.

Let me tell you how my father did his business.

He would never introduce himself as a salesman. We would come in together and I would scuttle myself away to some corner to pick and prod at some barrel or other and my father would be a customer.

He would ask for something small. A finger of butter if they had it or a button for his waistcoat, and he would count out the tin in his palm like it was the last pennies in both their worlds.

Transaction done my father would say, 'Let me show you something interesting, Mister Baker,' for he would be mindful to check the name above the door and use it as often as he felt necessary. He did not talk down to people when he was selling. Many salesmen take the road that they should be superior to their customer, that they are doing them a favor by speaking to them, and that the customer will buy from them because the salesman is letting them become as intelligent as they are by purchasing the goods they extol. This is particularly true if it is a luxurious or superfluous item that must be shown to be aspirational, especially if the customer is not wearing shoes.

You may have seen these salesmen in colorful coats and silk hats shouting at bumpkins about their cure-alls. They may wear a lined cape and carry a silver-topped cane. Mister Colt exemplified some of these manners but my father did not. I maintain that you do not trust a man whose shirt and pants are colorful and expensive. This man is out to impress first and does not wish to be measured by his words and actions but by appearance alone. Nature has the same rules. The most colorful and banded creatures are usually the most venomous. My father did not even wear a hat when we went west as he had done for those bustled city ladies with their reading-eye deficiencies. I did wear a hat but I was selling nothing and it was useful to hide my shyness under.

'Let me show you something interesting, Mister Baker,' and he would take out the wooden Colt from behind his back but hold it like a hammer rather than a gun so as to not alarm mister Baker.

'It is a new gun,' he would say. 'It is the pistol of the future, to be taken up by the army and navy. I have a note from President Jackson himself approving of the weapon.' At this juncture mister Baker would find the pistol in his hands, holding it for my father while he pulled out the copy of the note that indeed Colt had acquired from Old Hickory, no longer president but impressive all the same. It did not mean that the military approved of the gun, just that Colt had the sand to go to the capital and ask. As I told you: snake oil.

Mister Baker held the gun in his hand like a dead fish. 'It is made of wood, sir.' This was said in sympathy, as if my father was not aware of it and had been duped.

'It is a model. Now what do you suppose is so different about it?'

'It has no trigger.'

'It has a safety trigger. Cock the hammer, Mister Baker.'

He did so. A look of wonder as the cylinder wheeled into place with a click like a key in a lock and the trigger dropped in front of his finger. It would take a move of the digit to pass in front of the trigger, thus preventing unintentional fire. Now this rotating gun may seem an ordinary thing but not then. Collier's revolving flintlock and Allen's pepperbox were cranked by hand. This music-box action was as pleasing to the eye as to the ear.

'That is quite a trick!'

'What guns do you use yourself, Mister Baker?'

'I have my rifle, which I use with shot when I need.'

'It is a double?'

'It is.'

'And why would you use a double?'

Mister Baker being reeled in now by his own hand. 'For two shots, naturally.'

'Well, this gun will put five pistols in your hand and is rifled to boot.'

'A rifled pistol?'

'Accuracy and reliability is Samuel Colt's aim.'

Mister Baker passed back the gun. 'I have no want for a hand pistol.'

'I agree. We all know that the Allen gun with its multiple barrels is a top-heavy arm and is good for shooting a man across a table but is more likely to blow off your own hand. That is why it is only in small caliber and can barely stop a dog. The Colt patent however, if you notice'—the gun now back in mister Baker's hand— 'separates the chambers at such a distance that a loose spark from the percussion could never cause such a mishap and thus can come in a larger bore. It is not five shots to put a man down. It is one shot for five men or, as our army would have it—as the chambers do not have to be rotated with the other hand—ten shots for ten Comanche. A pistol in each fist.'

'That is all to the good. But I cannot afford a new gun.'

'No-one can, Mister Baker, that is true. Not when a gun is a lifetime's purchase. Samuel Colt is determined that good handguns should not be the luxury only of those who can afford craftsmanship. As you know, when you buy a gun it is made by one man. You must pay the price for that one man's dedication and ability, which can be a hefty sum. The Colt, however, is a machine-made arm. Its pieces are assembled by a team of men and, further, this means if it should fault through improper use, it can be repaired economically. No need to buy a new gun.'

'I cannot afford a new gun.' He cocked and fired the action. 'How much is it?'

This is also the mark of a good salesman. The price is the last thing on his mind. It is the value he sells, and now mister Baker knew the value of the weapon without seeing the price tag, which he may have judged unfairly.

'Mister Baker, I am heading west to put these guns into the hands of homesteaders. Colt wishes to bring defense into normal folks' lives. I am selling orders for these guns for you to make your own profit and I ask no money. Wholesale to yourself, and if you are kind enough to give my boy a twist of candy, I can let you have them for ten dollars each. Sell them at whatever you see right.'

'*Ten dollars?* A gun for ten dollars? Well, my!'

'For a twist of candy. And you can sell them for whatever you see right. I can let you have one right now for yourself for eight, take your order for the rest, and I will be on my way.'

'Well, that is an attraction!'

My father took out his order book and licked his pencil.

There was a low laugh from the end of the store.

Mister Baker's store was L-shaped. He had tables at the back so as no ladies would feel intimidated. This was where men drank and gambled cards or bone-sticks. It was dark. I had not noticed it was there.

'Haw, haw, Chet!' A chair went back. 'I can sell you a wooden knife too if you wants it, Chet Baker!' He came out of the dark. I stepped sideways toward my father.

My father turned to the sound of the boots.

'It is a model, sir. I promise the real. It is steel.'

The man was brought into the light now as if the

23

darkness had pushed him out of it. He was brown all the way down. From his wool hat to his boots he was dirty and baked. His face bearded and black; only the whites of his eyes, which were wide, defined it. I could smell his drink then. It was not yet one o'clock. He had two closed flapped holsters angled on his black belt.

'You say ten dollars for one of them guns, mister?'

'That is wholesale, sir. And a special price for mister Baker.' My father did not know how to speak to these people. 'Twenty dollars for a belt model and that will get you a box and spare cylinder and loading-tool, sir.'

The man grinned. 'Don't call me *sir*, you little shit.'

Mister Baker knew how to speak to them.

'Now, Thomas.' I blinked that this creature had my name. 'Get back and I will be right over once I am done. I am trading here. Do not fool with my day or it will be the last you drink here.'

Thomas leaned on his hip, thumbed his belt. The flap on the holster nearest my father was not buttoned.

'I would like to see one of them guns. I heard everything you said, salesman. I am an interested party.'

There was a childish giggle back in the dark. Another man who had not come up.

Thomas rubbed his nose at the laugh and showed only the top of his dusty hat as he lowered his face so we would not see it smiling. He flashed it up again.

'Now see, I have me one of them pepperbox pistols that you disparaged so much, salesman. I have it in the back of me. You say it is small and would not stop a dog. What say we try it up against one of these horseshit pistols of yours? See what dog does what.'

I looked at my father but dared not move closer lest

24

this Thomas mistook me in the gloom for a man of intent.

My father did not look to me but held a palm out for me to stay. I wanted to go home. Would run if I had to.

'I do not have them with me. They are in my hotel.'

'Well, surely we should test it? Would you not agree? If I am to buy something, I think that that is fair. And my friend Chet there should see it too before he parts with his tin. Is that not right, Chet?'

Mister Chet Baker shook his head. 'Thomas Heywood, you are making me regret letting you in here. I will buy what I want to buy without your say!'

Thomas stepped forward. 'You got any gun on you, salesman?'

My father did not hold with guns. He turned to mister Baker. 'I will come back in the morning, Mister Baker. We can sign up then.' He picked up the wooden gun, put it slowly back to his belt, and held out his hand to me and said my name, which drew the other Thomas' eye to me for the first time. I saw that my father's hand trembled and ran to it.

Thomas threw down. 'Don't you turn your back on me, you son of a bitch!'

A single-shot percussion, too small for its holster. A belt gun with a short barrel. The under-hammer type where you just pulled the trigger and it fired. No man who had dollars to buy a gun had one. I doubted he had that pepperbox also. But I did not think that gun so little then. It was a cannon pointed to my father's back.

There was the giggle again from the black rear. It

25

sounded like it came from a short, fat throat. I still had faith that mister Baker was in charge of this room. He had said that he had a double-shot rifle and I hoped it was as much of his workplace as his apron.

My father gripped my hand and did something that I did not understand then.

I have made my peace with it.

He switched from holding my hand and squeezed both my shoulders and put me in front of his waist, in front of the gun.

'Please,' he said. 'My boy?'

The gun stared at me with its innocent Cyclops eye and swallowed me whole, a chasm before me. My father behind.

'*Please,*' he said again.

I cannot remember how he said it but in my mind it sounded like the 'Amen' that people say too loud in church for show to their neighbors rather than in devotion.

Thomas Heywood roared, buckled over with a callous glee. When he came back up his fist was empty, the flap of his holster closed.

'Run, you son of a bitch!' He rolled back with laughter, the dust blowing off him like a cloud. I saw that his coat was made out of a blanket and sewn with wide stitches like sharks' teeth.

My father pulled me away and out the door with that laugh at our backs.

We did not run. We left briskly. Everyone else on the street was just slow.

FIVE

That night we stayed in a room on Front street above a potter's called Bastian. This was two dollars for a brass bed but no meal. I figured my father was of the opinion that the man named Thomas Heywood would not spend two dollars for a room so would not likely be one of our neighbors. We had moved our belongings from the hotel along with the sack of guns. I carried the three boxed models like books under my chin. I did not complain about the weight.

In the room my father moved the kerosene lamp from the window and put it on the floor and drew the curtain. We ate salt-beef sandwiches and sauerkraut from a newspaper on the bed with the lamp throwing grotesque shadows of us on the ceiling like a Chinese silhouette show. We did not talk.

I had wanted my father to come into the room, lock the door, and laugh and slap his thigh about how lucky we had been and how foolish the whole scene was to civilized folks like us, but he did not. He had hid the lamp and chewed quietly in case the mice heard him. I could hear his watch tick.

In bed that night a piano along the street tickled me awake and I found myself alone under the blankets.

The lamp was down and flickering, the whole room dancing around the walls.

I was just about to lift up when there was a rattle like someone at our door lock and I froze. Then I was fully awake and knew the sound of the knob on our door turning was inside the room. The stranger twisting the lock was the clockwork and snaps of a gun.

I sat up but my father did not notice as he had the chair faced to the wall and his head down. I saw the box of one of the belt models open on the floor. On the green baize lid was a waxed paper image of the factory with smoke billowing from the chimneys. The inserts where the pistol and its accoutrements lay were skeletal empty. Mister Colt had provided us with caps and balls to demonstrate. Powder too. The boxes held cartridge paper, dowel, and block, and these were on the side table. When they were in their box, in their proper neat holes, they looked like a carpenter's or an artist's tools. They fooled you that they could create.

I went to speak but the hammer's double click shushed me. That sound cuts you down to be quiet. It silences giants, and only dumb animals roar at it.

It has committal.

My father whispered from his corner.

'Forgive me, Jane. My sweetest friend. What I . . . Oh, Jane, it was . . . Preserve me. My sweetest friend.' He took a breath and the piano down the street stopped and people clapped and laughed. He quoted to the wall with that breath.

'"Long is the way, and hard, that out of Hell leads up to light."'

I threw back the bedclothes and he turned to me.

'Thomas?' he said. 'I thought you were asleep.' He uncocked the gun. Pistols do this reluctantly.

I ran from the bed and around the chair. The gun was in his lap and his arms wrapped around me. I felt the pistol's coldness against my belly through my shirt. He patted me closer and my cheek touched his, which was damp.

'Oh, my boy . . . my boy.' He chuckled and it was the nicest music.

You may have had a father or you may have had a man who lived in your house. If he beat you or left you I will suffer you that and if you carry it with you then you can have some pity. But I saw my father's shame and he passed it on to me. If he had hit me I could abide, I could overcome. The Lord does these things so we do not do it ourselves. This is how man changes his generations, the way birds move on from barren lands, and we abide.

I told you when I started that my life began when I was twelve. It was there in that room. I did not exist before that night and I am still that boy.

He held me away. 'I was only loading the gun so I could learn. So I could show Mister Baker in the morning.' Then, as if to avow to himself rather than settle me, 'I am sure that man will not be there then. We will do our business and be gone with Jude Brown.'

'We could go home,' I said.

'We could. But there is no need, Tom. We will be on the road tomorrow. Everything will be well. Here, let me show you how fast I can load this thing. It is a marvel, I swear.'

I wiped my eyes and he rubbed his, lamenting his tiredness and concentration. I noticed he had only loaded one chamber.

I watched him play the gun like that piano outside. The gun in its simplicity and pleasing mechanics coaxed confidence from his hands; it forgave the amateur. And there was the V cut into the hammer as a back sight, the blade at the end of the octagonal barrel, and if you lined them up, aimed your eye down that V, down that steel-barreled extension of your arm, you would shoot the thing in front of you. But the gun does not know how to pull the trigger.

I did not ask him why he could not have practiced with the wooden gun. It separated and loaded just the same and even had wooden caps and balls. I never thought of it, or why the loaded gun did not go back to its green baize bed.

SIX

We packed and fetched the Brewster and Jude Brown first thing. Jude Brown was reluctant to leave either the food or the company of horses although as a gelding they should have smelled like dogs to him. We rode to Baker's in silence. My father did not tip his head to anyone, which was not his custom and a bad habit for a salesman. His little gold glasses kept slipping down his nose with his sweat and he was forever confusing Jude Brown by lifting the reins to set them glasses right.

Baker's reached, my father jumped down. I had no will to follow but still he said, 'Wait here.'

He took two naked belt guns, whose barrels were about five inches, made for as they sounded, and he intimated such by tucking one in his belt.

'I will not be long.' He slapped the reins into my hand.

31

I watched the door close and looked at the back of Jude Brown's head so as not to meet the eye of anyone on the street. There was a black boy in cotton-duck overalls on the porch sweeping but with no intention on cleaning. He was moving the dust around with the strength of a marionette and studied me and Jude Brown. I played the reins through my fingers and looked up at the mountains covered in cloud, the endless trees on them in the early morning still blue-green like the sea. It was not yet ten. I would not think that a man like Thomas Heywood had got out of his filthy bed by now.

I could not help but look at the door once or twice and each time the black boy grinned a gapped mouth. I chiseled my face like a man with fury in him. I did not truck with boys. I had a wagon and a horse. I had a sack full of guns. I dipped my hat to a milkmaid who instead of smiling or blushing looked at me scornfully. I pulled the brim down as if this was originally my intention.

I do not know how long I sat but it seemed as if the whole world passed by, their clothes getting smarter with every minute as the work they traveled to shifted from strong back to desk and pen, for the earlier you have to get up the harder you have to work. My father was taking his time. I thought on the two guns he had taken in and then I could think of nothing else except Thomas Heywood's white, wide eyes.

The door and its bell exploded like a gunshot and I jumped, which made Jude Brown toss his head and curse me with a snort when nothing happened. My father was there and shaking mister Baker's hand. He climbed up onto the seat and took the reins, adjusting them tighter where I had been running them through my hands.

He snapped Jude Brown off and the black boy smiled good-bye and waved us away with a wide, pendulous swing as if hailing a raft from the shore to warn of white water ahead.

We left Milton at the west end and there were more tents outside here than coming in and skinny dogs barked at us, danced at Jude Brown, bit at our wheels then wagged their tails back to their masters proud that they had seen us off.

A great weight lifted off me that I did not know was there. Later we were talking again and pointing out jaybirds. My father had taken an order for six pistols and sold one for mister Baker's own use. At dinner he put back the pistol from his belt to the wagon. He could not unload it, as is the way with guns (they only empty one way), but he said that would not be to any detriment.

'It will be provident if we see us a rabbit.' He smiled but it had no weight to it and my smile back was even lighter.

We had a new plan for our journey. We would head south, follow the mountains, to make the Cumberland road. This was the national road, as you may recall, a redbrick toll road that would carry us safely through the mountains and west into Illinois. It closed in '38, I believe, when the money ran out or the road ran out, whichever is truer. Over six hundred miles long, and the trail to get down there would add three or four days onto our month, Cumberland being near two hundred miles. But the thought of a good and busy road with civilized turnpikes was comforting. It was the sensible thing to do. Getting there, however, in the shadow of the mountains would be rough country.

We crossed the Susquehanna at Lewis, where we took a cooked supper but did no business, keen as my father was to get on and leave Milton far behind. This was a pity as Lewis seemed like a bustling, money-heavy borough.

With mister Baker's eight dollars for a pistol and even with our expenses we now had us thirty-two dollars. My father was a good accountant. Already the trip had turned profit.

We camped under the mountains and as it grew dark I looked up into the trees and saw the friendly glow of other travelers' fires like the tips of cigars, a thousand feet above, separated by miles of forest. The mountains were alive and I did not feel lonely. And I was with my father and he was happier now.

'If we are up with the sun I reckon we could make Huntingdon by tomorrow evening,' he said. 'I will do some business and get us a bed there. We shall need a good sleep. It will be another two days before we can get to Cumberland.'

We spoke like we were mountain men, as if we followed the stars and that two hundred miles were just stepping-stones across a creek. If we were real foresters we would have followed the creeks and the mills and seen towns we did not know existed. But our Brewster would have been no good along a creek. These trails as

34

they were did not do too much to improve its wooden springs.

'Could we not sell the wagon?' I inquired. 'Get another horse? We might travel quicker.'

He looked at me harshly and I blushed. This had been my mother's wagon. 'You are too young to ride. And I would be worried about bears if we did not have the cart to sleep on.'

I had not thought about bears and I looked about into the trees and made sure that I did not rattle the pot or my spoon as I ate the Indian meal.

Night, and the sparrows and tanagers had ceased nagging us to get out. We had only a middling fire left with white coals and chars of wood. I could see nothing except my father and the shape of Jude Brown standing like a statue in the dark. I was not tired and my father insisted on one more enamel mug of tea and he drove a stick through the coals and put our mugs directly on them.

The coals sparked and I watched them sparks drift up like angry wasps. My neck went back to follow them to the stars and I missed the men step out of the trees. When I came back to earth they were there like they had always been with us, as if they were the trees we had thought our walls.

Four of them. In surtout coats like old soldiers and wide wool hats. Each had a rifle in his hand and belt tied outside his coat with flap holsters or pistols tied by lanyards. They had made a circle around us. They were bearded and dark below their hats although I could see that one had shaved silver hair close about his ears and a fat mustache. I saw this because he was at my side like a giant. I was sat cross-legged, tailor-wise, and I looked down from his face to his boots. They did not match or one had been fished out of a river.

My father had rolled up and stood with his hands raised. No-one had asked him to do this.

'What do you want?' he asked.

It was too dark to see clearly, as the voice that answered was in front of the dying fire to me, but I knew it at once.

'All that you have, salesman.' It was Thomas Heywood.

'You can have it,' my father said. 'I do not want trouble.'

'You give me trouble, salesman? Is that what you said?' Thomas threw down again, only with a proper pistol this time, a good Ketland percussion. He punctuated his words with its terrible click.

There was the fat giggle again from near Thomas and I could just make out that this would be the man from Chet Baker's store. He had an old face that should have known better, with a grizzled, rough shave like he plucked his beard with tweezers. He was short and threw down also. He had a hat with a beaded band like something of an Indian decoration. He grinned with teeth the whole time as if he were showing them to a surgeon. I could not see the fourth man at all other than his raised rifle. He was all in black with a high collar to hide him.

'No. I will give no trouble,' my father said, and took off his spectacles and folded them into his waistcoat. I do not know why he did this. It would blur them all. At my mother's funeral he had also taken them off but I thought that for vanity.

'I hear the word *trouble* again, salesman.' Heywood came closer. 'You keep saying that word, salesman. Do you like that word?'

I hold that my father did not know how to speak to these men.

'What do you want?' he asked.

'Am I repeating myself again?' Heywood came yet closer, he and my father like bride and groom. 'All you have, I said, didn't I?' He lowered his gun, looked at his trash around us. 'But first I want you to show me how much you love that horseshit pistol of yours. I want you to get that pistol, salesman.'

I suppose now that they had followed us from Milton. Our Brewster would have left marks. They had probably drunk in a saloon in Lewis while we ate and maybe they had kept an eye on Jude Brown and our Brewster on the street. Their wickedness planned with laughter and rum. The banality of evil is in the joviality of the simpleminded.

'Get yourself a pistol, salesman.'

My father looked over to me.

Heywood laughed. 'Oh, see him, boys!' He waved the pistol to my direction. 'Go on, salesman. *Go on!* Grab your boy in front again! Bet yourself that I won't shoot through him!'

The others laughed as cowards laugh around a bully. These men had no wives or children or work that paid. Nothing but themselves. They were children more than I. Their violence and reasoning the same as children, only with lead now instead of sticks, and if there had been no lead or steel it would be sticks still. Everything my father said would be wrong. I had seen boys like this when I backed away from our windows at home. My father could not win. He was me backing away from the laughter in the street.

'Get your pistol, salesman.' Thomas lifted his cocked gun and the giggle from Indian-hatband came again.

My father straightened up. 'If I take it, you will shoot me, or your men will shoot me. If I leave it you will shoot me and take everything anyway. So why not just rob me and be done. And me and my boy will leave these mountains. We will go home, I assure you. We will go home. I am done now.'

'Rob you? *Rob you?* Am I a thief now, is it? Are you saying I would shoot you and rob you without a chance? Is that what I am? Am I that low in your eyes?' He was mad now. It was done.

'No,' my father said. 'It is whatever you want. I will tell no-one. Just let me and my boy go. Take the wagon and the horse and we will walk out of here now and you gentlemen can have it all.' He moved toward me with his head down, his back to Heywood.

'You turn your back on me again, you son of a bitch?'

And that was it.

Thomas Heywood fired into my father's back with a snap of his wrist like throwing a stone. Like nothing. It flashed and sparked like the fire just minutes before and the trees quaked. I think I cried out. My father fell to his knees and disturbed our mugs in the fire, which sputtered with the tea and coals and startled the others to unload into him, their guns lighting the trunks of the trees four more times, Heywood emptying another pistol, and Jude Brown raised his hooves and tried to jump from his tether.

He still whinnied and snorted as my father lay still and the dark came back like a lamp snuffed. Indian-hatband giggled again.

I had never seen the top of my father's head before. He was going bald. It is foolish how you notice these things.

You may have heard that the dead twitch and jerk as they go on and they may, but I had been saved from that sight. My father simply fell and lay like a cut log, only the dust from his fall showing that he had weight. He had no more movement. His neck was angled and his arms were underneath him, his shoes pointed together.

'You want the horse?' asked the man who had left my side as if I was not there.

'Why would I want a horse with no dick?' Heywood said. 'Leave the wagon. Get the guns and the money. Take it all. Leave the boy and the ground.'

The hatband giggler stopped his mirth. 'Leave the boy?'

'He's a boy. Get moving.'

I do not think this was mercy.

I had not stirred past looking at the top of my father's head. I watched the silver-haired man take Father's watch and purse and kick him back over again. Someone rubbed Jude Brown's nose and he settled down while they robbed the wagon. There was laughter at the discovery of the wooden gun and they threw it on my father's back.

I did not notice them leaving. They said nothing to me and just melted away.

I sat in the dark for a half hour, I guess. Jude Brown tried to talk to me. He just wanted to know that everything was all right, so at some time I stood up and rubbed his neck. I sat up on the Brewster and played his reins through my fingers.

I sat there for hours listening to the owls and the forest creaking, watching shooting stars and hearing things snuffling just outside our camp. Branches fall at night, did you know that? You can be sitting in silence and suddenly something falls and you jump.

Eventually false dawn came and I got down and went to our tin of char cloth and striker. I made a fire. There were flying insects everywhere, even on my hands as I sparked and they did not care. I pulled out the cups from the ash and drank what was in them. They had taken the oven pot.

My father's body gurgled but I knew he was not alive. After an hour I rolled him over. I recognized nothing about him, and in a way this was easier to me. His mouth was open and bloodied wet and his eyes stared up. I tried to close them but they would not. I tried to close his mouth but his teeth just ground and it flopped back open. It felt like rubbing a brick against another and the feeling of it through my arm made me throw up my belly.

I went through his pockets and got just his compass and spectacles. I picked up the wooden Paterson and stuffed it in my belt. They had tossed away my father's order book and I stooped and plucked each one of the white paper chits like picking cotton and placed them back.

Dawn now and the birds tried to get rid of me again

with their cries. I knew I could not pick up his body. I was not strong enough. I have had to live with that.

I covered him with our blankets, not thinking of the next night, and me and Jude Brown went back the way we came.

I did not cry. Not once. It is very important for you to know that. I would not get anywhere with crying. I wooed Jude Brown and clucked when I wanted him to get along. I do not think he cared anything about what had happened and he stopped when we cleared into wide ground until I fed him. He took an age with his bag, and I chewed corn dodgers for breakfast and waited for him. There was no satisfaction in my eating. I could taste nothing.

When I got back up onto the seat my feet touched the loaded Paterson that my father had practiced with. He had left it underneath and it had moved as I rode. Heywood had not seen it. I took out the wooden one and put it at my feet and put this steel one in its place. Jude Brown took us to a creek and I had to untie him to let him drink. I washed for I had the smell of gunpowder and smoke all over.

I would go back to Milton, back to mister Baker. He knew me and my father. That would do for now.

SEVEN

I had done back through Lewis and on to Milton. It had taken the best part of the day and the town had gone quiet for suppertime when I reached Baker's store. Mercifully he was still open. I put the guns in the sofkee bag and hid it under the seat.

I hesitated before my hand reached the door. I realized I had not spoken to anyone since last night and that I had not thought of what I was to say or why I was to say it. I was childishly embarrassed. I was used to not piping up when I got the small piece of pie, to be thankful for the warm buttermilk. I sat quietly in corners and let adults talk. But I knew I needed the company and security of good men. I would say it all just as it was. They would know the right thing to do and I would go back to sitting quietly in corners while they made the world right again. I opened the door.

Mister Baker was behind his counter, I doubted if the town recognized him without a bar of wood in front of him. He stopped wiping something and fixed me with a questioning look, then recalled me and looked over my head for my father's shape. I had frozen in the doorway for I had heard lewd laughter and the chime of glass from the dark area. I had not thought on the possibility that I was coming back into the den where I had first seen beasts.

The change in me had not gone unnoticed and mister Baker came closer to me along his counter.

'What is it, son?'

I took off my hat and stepped up to the brass rail along the foot of the bar.

'My father,' I said. My voice was dry and I swallowed to moisten my throat but I had nothing in me to wet it. 'He has been shot and killed. I would like to go home now.'

Mister Baker had no wife but he found a neighbor who held me tight to her bosom when she heard and gave me a good stew and dumplings, which I did prefer more. She had no children, which was to the good. I would not know how to address myself to them now, my usual shyness of other children presently deepened by my horrors. She called me 'dear' at every word and made me a cot in her parlor. I kept the sofkee bag with the guns beside me.

I was a little fearful when mister Baker left to take care of Jude Brown but I comforted myself that he was only across the street. The neighbor did not leave me a light when she 'deared' me good night, which at first worried me, but I realized that no-one would have reason to look in through the window of a darkened room. Before settling I got out from under the four-patch quilt and checked the locks on the windows. I slept a little. I dreamed a lot. I do not want to write about them dreams.

There was no law in Milton. That would come when they got a post office. The bank had men on a payroll of a dollar and a half a day to protect its interests and they could be persuaded to keep order on a Saturday night. Mister Baker informed me in the morning after he had opened and set me down in a chair with my bag by my feet that we would have to apply to a judge in Lewisburg and make Thomas Heywood a matter for the marshals.

I dreaded the concept of repeating my entire story to a man in black who did not know my father from a hole in the ground but I trusted mister Baker as a man who had at least conversed and traded with my father. He was kin to me now. Even today every shop-keeper reminds of him whenever I see a white apron and cuff protectors. I have found most of them to be polite and warm. They are the few of us who often see all walks of life and unlike with a doctor or a lawman it is mostly a happy event when someone purchases something, and they meet us at our best, which must be good for their souls. They become the begrudging kind when they have been taken advantage of or stolen from too often. I have met these also.

The evil men who had done this to me had left me with Jude Brown and our Brewster and our clothes. I had no money in the world and was dependent on strangers. I expressed to mister Baker that I wanted to get back to New York.

'What about your father's body, Thomas?' he asked. 'Would you not like to give him a Christian burial?'

I thought on the blankets I had left over my father's body. I thought on the snuffling and howls of unseen things.

'I would like that, sir, but . . . it has been some time . . . and it will be more time to get back to . . .'

Bless mister Chet Baker. I saw my uncompleted thoughts trawl across his face. I had burdened him with my dilemmas unfairly. I had asked to go home and now this poor man had to spend part of his precious day considering my future, which had walked into his store. A good shopkeeper finds it hard to say no. As I understand it, in China, if one walks into a store and asks for something that the store does not stock, rather than say no and disappoint, that little Chinaman will keep nodding and bringing out things that you may like instead. I guess mister Baker was of this tradition. *No* was not a word for him.

The bell broke our cabal and I jumped at the door swinging wide. A tall man blew in and hung holding the door as if Odysseus had returned. He had a gray greatcoat that did not suit the warmer weather that April was bringing. He looked at mister Baker and me like furniture and walked to the counter with a grunt.

He wore a weak hat that could have been his grandpa's for it certainly looked older than him but his beard made him older. He could have been seventy with them whiskers. He had those same black-flapped holsters around his belt that I had come to fear and smaller ones that probably held just as terrifying devices.

'I have a list, Chet, if you please,' he said, and occupied the counter with a great familiarity as if he owned the place.

Mister Baker tapped my knee and stood and brushed his hands down his apron. He went to his stage. The man looked back at me with a cocked head and sniffed and turned away.

'Right with you, Henry.' Mister Baker's voice was friendly and I relaxed a bit. He took the list and perused it with a squint. I guessed the man to have bad script. 'Are you stopping a spell, Henry?'

'No, I am not,' the man said. 'I am on to Cherry Hill. They may have some loose prisoners to fetch. Men like to escape for the summer. Let me try your jerky.'

Mister Baker handed him a strip of the beef that was strung on a cord above and the man leaned on the counter and surveyed the room and me.

I knew of Cherry Hill. This was the Philadelphia state prison shaped like a wagon's wheel. It was the largest jail in America and freshly built. Pennsylvania was famous throughout the world for its efficiency of handling criminals for reform and punishment, and the Pennsylvania system of separate confinement would become the model for the world. It even had flush toilets in each cell. Even President Buren did not have one of those, although with the state of the country he had gained from Jackson he probably had need of it.

46

My face must have lit up at the sound of places close to home for this man Henry studied me more.

'You making opinion on me, boy?'

'No, sir.'

He snorted and went back to his business. 'I have tobacco twists to sell, Chet. Virginian. Don't want to take it with me.'

'I know, I know, Henry.' Mister Baker waved him down and went about with his cans and bags to the counter. 'Store-pay or coin?'

'What you will. What is with the boy, Chet? You a wet nurse now?'

On this morning I had no opinion on Henry Stands. He was of those rough-and-ready, broad, fat men we tended to elect as presidents and senators when they were too old to do anything else and too ornery to lie down. He had that same military bearing and attitude of patience that they had seen it all and leaned on the seasons like fences and watched the rest of the world cluck and run around.

Mister Baker stopped in his actions and lowered his voice. 'His father has been killed. Not two days gone.'

'Killed by who?' I still think that a strange, direct questioning.

'Thomas Heywood. He was working on the canal building last I knew. Do you know him?'

'I do not.' Henry Stands turned back to me. 'You are not hurt, boy?'

'No, sir. It was not just Heywood. There was four of them.'

'Where is your mother?'

'The pock took my mother last year.'

47

Mister Baker seemed to sink. 'I did not know that. I am sorry, son.'

Henry bit off more jerky and spoke through his chewing. 'So you are an orphan now, boy?'

This had not occurred to me. But it was true. An orphan.

'I cannot say,' I said, and meant it. 'I have my house with my aunt.'

'My, Chet, you have inherited a piece. What's your name, boy?'

'Thomas Walker, sir.'

'Henry Stands.' And that was his introduction. 'Thomas Walker.' He said my name as if he were chewing on it to see if it was something he should swallow or spit. 'You hold the same name as the man that done this? That is unfortunate. Well, boy, there is no shame in being an orphan. I am an orphan myself. That is because I am old and that is what happens. You may become a smarter man than me as it has come to you so young.' He rubbed his nose. 'I am sorry for your loss. I'll take tea, Chet, and rum if you has it in half bottles or I will take gin.' He turned away.

'Henry? You are heading east. Could it not be available that you could take the boy with? He is of New York.'

Henry bit off more jerky. 'I am not to New York. I am to Philadelphia.'

Although I had not yet formed my views on Henry Stands I saw an opportunity to leave this place, and right soon, for this man was set to leaving and that suited me.

I stood up. 'I am not to New York. I am for Paterson, New Jersey.'

48

They both looked at me. 'Mister Samuel Colt is expecting me there.' I knew how to catch this old goat. 'He has monies for me. We have business. I can pay.'

'What's he jawing about?'

'His father was selling guns. I bought half a dozen myself on promise and one for my own.' He reached below. 'Now see this here.' The Paterson came out. Henry took it by the barrel and reversed it into his palm quicker than I could see. He weighed it smartly.

'Should be brassed. It'll rust like nails.' He half cocked it and watched the cylinder click round and the trigger drop. 'That is pretty.' But he said this with scorn. He took it all the way and the cylinder finished its trick. It was not loaded but he did not fire; such action can damage the placings for the caps. He let the hammer back. This was an experienced man.

'It does not load down the barrel? How is it to be done?' He tugged down on the barrel. 'Does it snap? I fear I will break it and owe you, Chet.'

I stepped across.

'I will show you, sir.' I held out my hand for the gun. Henry Stands grunted and passed it over. I half cocked it again and showed him the key wedge on the barrel. 'This taps out,' I said, and did it exactly as my father had shown me using the pocket compass as a hammer. 'You can pull the barrel right off.' I did and placed it on the counter. 'This makes it perfect for cleaning or for buying longer barrels for greater accuracy. Now you can take the cylinder off the arbor and load the chambers. The arbor will double as a ram for the shot in a pinch or you can use your own tool or the one supplied, which fits through this slot in the arbor.' I assembled the gun again with my father's hands.

'You can load all five chambers and keep a cap on four. The hammer will rest on an empty nipple for safety if you so choose but the chamber will be loaded ready.' I eased the hammer down and put it back in his hand. 'With spare cylinders you can load fast and have five shots in moments.'

'Spare?'

'For more dollars it comes with a spare and tool, cutter, cartridge maker, nipple picker, and twenty-two-grain loader.'

'Does it come with pan and brush to pick up the pieces when it chain-fires? I never seen so many screws. Who made this toy?'

'Mister Samuel Colt of the Patent Arms Manufacturing Company, sir,' I declared straight up.

'You paid for this, Chet?'

'And ordered six more, Henry.' He winked at me.

'You shoot it yet?'

'I only had it a day, Henry.'

'Do you want to buy a unicorn as well, Chet?'

'I seen a letter from Jackson affirming it.'

'I have an affidavit for my unicorn from the same hand. Ink still wet.' He put his first finger on the mouth of the barrel. 'I have nothing under a musket-bore. Make me a load, Chet, twenty-two-grain like the boy says. We'll go out back and see what this Indian gun can do. I can get by with one hand if she goes grenado on me.'

Mister Baker set up a plank of pine against the back fence. This was maybe thirty yards from Henry Stands, who stood, feet apart, playing the pistol back and forth in his hands. I would admit that the gun looked weak in his fists.

'You clear out now, Chet. No telling what this thing will do.'

Mister Baker dodged back and came beside me. I watched Henry Stands take a breath, which also appeared to move something unpleasant in his chest, which he spat out. He puffed his chest again and I failed to notice mister Baker cover his ears, and a blink later I was deaf.

The gun-smoke was pure white. A waft of copper and hot iron and a puff of sawdust from the plank. I thought of the five shots into my father. Two from Heywood. I had not heard their noise.

Once down from the frame the trigger stayed until the shooter put it back. This allowed for rapid fire and Henry Stands picked up on this a breath later and blasted twice more successively.

He was now in a cloud and I wondered how he could see or even think as my hands were clapped to my ears and I was dizzy.

He shifted his footing and, as there is only one tidy way to empty any firearm, he cracked it twice more into the suffering wood.

Five shots like the ticking of a watch. He stepped out of his cloud.

'Well.' He turned the gun over, looking on it. 'It did not blow to pieces. That is a good thing. It would benefit from a guard for the trigger to rest as you pull for the next shot. I guess palming it with the other hand would make for better accuracy. That makes it useless from a horse.'

51

I piped up. 'If you had thinner fingers it would not be a problem. It has no guard or exposed trigger to make its first draw smooth and fast.'

'And slip from your hand like a fish,' he said.

Mister Baker was at the plank. 'You have almost split it, Henry! Five holes in five seconds!'

I looked perhaps too conceitedly at Henry Stands. 'It is five pistols in the hand, sir!'

'Is that a fact.' He did not look at the wood and its holes but I saw that they covered not much more than three fingers. 'Is that a fact,' he repeated, and put the gun to his belt and strode back into the store with a pace that did not ask us to follow. The bell on the door went. Mister Baker shrugged at me and walked to my part of the yard. He was about to speak when the bell shook once more and we heard the stomp of Henry's boots across the boards and he appeared with a rifle under his arm.

'Mister Baker?' I asked. 'Who is this man?'

'I know he was an Indiana ranger,' mister Baker whispered.

'Is he a good man?'

'Well . . .' We watched Henry Stands put the rifle to his shoulder and aim at the wood. 'He likes the sound of guns.'

The rifle cocked with three clicks and I muffled my ears again. He fired but there was no explosion or white smoke or any other smoke. There was only a crack like dropping a book on a parquet floor. Then Henry Stands without a pause cocked and fired again and then—*a miracle!*—he fired again, and then again, and once more, at which he stopped, for the plank was now kindling.

Without smoke or fire or cannon it seemed as if the action of Henry Stands had no relation to the destruction of the wood. It was his stare that broke it.

He nodded, satisfied, and lowered the magical weapon. He came and glared over me, presented the rifle in front of me like a scepter of office. I saw that it had an oddly bulbous stock.

'Your Mister Colt has invented the spinning wheel again. This gun is as old as I. I have twenty-two shots. I have an infantry. I need no powder or fulminate and she does not foul. I am alive because of it.' He swung it back under his arm and tossed the Colt back to mister Baker. 'Good luck selling those pieces, Chet. Now, we done with business? I will get out before some widow tries to wed me.' He went back into the store with mister Baker at his heels. I came after, disheartened and amazed equally. My ears were plugged like I was underwater.

EIGHT

The rifle clattered on the counter. Mister Baker was back at his trade, Henry Stands complaining that he had overestimated what he could carry and separating random goods with a swipe of his arm.

'I have a wagon,' I said. 'If you take me to Paterson, New Jersey, you may have use of it.'

'I carry what I need. I am not a snail to carry my house with me. How much do I owe, Chet? Less the sack of tobacco I will give.'

Mister Baker began to tally up. I did not wish to harry his pencil but at the bottom of his page was the hope of my leaving.

'Mister Stands?' I brought out from my coat the order book. 'I have a responsibility to return to Mister Samuel Colt the orders my father took. Including six pistols for your friend, good Mister Baker here. Mister Colt will pay on receipt of those orders.'

Mister Baker looked to me to quiet, but I carried on. 'After my father's deposit and Mister Colt's commission, that will be seventy-five dollars owed to me. That is no awful sum for a few days' work and you are going east anyways.' I offered over the book but he did not move.

'This Colt will pay in specie? I ain't no use for shinplaster.'

I did not know how mister Colt would pay, but that lack of knowledge would not help me. 'We have a contract.'

'Is that signed by Jackson too?' He snorted and pulled out a drawstring bag. 'How much, Chet?'

Mister Baker looked sorry at me. 'You can have it gratis if you take the boy, Henry.'

'You telling me what to do, Chet?'

'No, Henry. I'm trading. The boy's no good to me here.'

Henry slammed down three coins. Mexican silver. 'I'll get your tobacco.' He took up his scant goods and his rifle. 'Open the door, boy.'

I hesitated and he also. Mister Baker indicated the door with a serious glare and I dashed and opened it. The sight of Henry Stands's big horse gave me an idea about my own. I followed down the porch.

'I am east and you are east. I could follow you. I'm sure once you split for Cherry Hill I could make my way on my own. I will be no burden.'

He began to load up. 'You are burdening me now.'

'You cannot stop me from following you.'

He gave a mean look from over the saddle. 'I can stop you.'

I needed to change my reasoning. 'How is it that your gun works?'

He continued tying and tightening the straps and bags of his horse. 'It is a wind-rifle. It uses air.'

'I have never seen anything like it.'

'And you never shall.' He had stopped looking at me as he spoke.

'Where did you get it?'

'I took it from a man.'

'Mister Baker says you were an Indiana ranger.'

He swung up on his black horse. 'I was.'

'What is the name of your horse?'

'He has none. Would be wrong to be forced to eat something that had a name.' He reached behind and swung a sack to me. 'Here. Give that to Chet. Good luck to you, boy.' He set off slow.

I called to his back, 'I only want to go home!'

He rolled his head back to me. He was already past the porch. 'You sure about that?'

I grabbed the stinking bag and ran back inside. I dropped it on the counter, suddenly breathless. 'Mister Baker, I thank you for your kindness. Is Jude Brown at the hostler?'

'He is.'

'I will deduct from your order his bill if you will give me one of those Mexican coins for him now.'

'Hold on, son. What now . . .?'

I ran for my sack. I would leave my clothes. 'Mister Stands is going to wait for me there. He has seen the value in escorting me.'

56

Mister Baker wanted to speak some more. I could tell I was not to get my coin. 'Never mind.' I ran but stopped at the door. 'I will see that you get your guns, Mister Baker.'

'No mind. I ain't in a hurry to settle bills.'

He called out after me but I did not hear what his concern was. I ran to the hostler with the sack banging at my knees. Henry Stands was shrinking along the road. The white bedroll at his back gleamed in the sun. I could follow that.

Jude Brown was pleased to see me and was still hitched to the Brewster. *Thank God!* The hostler was a bald free black man in a leather apron and wicker hat. I thought of lying to him that mister Baker would pay him later but I did not know what powers black men have to tell when boys are lying. I went into my sack. I had the wooden gun and the one real and my father's spectacles. They were gold-rimmed, worth four dollars anywhere. They still had his finger smudges.

The hostler was happy enough to take the real gun and so he should! A pistol for some green grain and water!

I cracked Jude Brown out of there and rattled up the road. I could not see Henry Stands but that would change. I was defenseless without that gun but considered I would not have been able to use it anyways bar to hurt myself; besides, leaving it had reason. I would now need company to be secure on the trail home. If I had sold the spectacles for the grain I might have been mistaken that the gun could protect, eased a little with its counterfeit confidence, and not chased Henry Stands so ardent.

As it was I had no money, no habiliments, some food, and a wooden gun to the good when I came across some wooden Indians.

I left that part of the Appalachians having never crossed them. The west still a mystery and you can keep it. Jude Brown and I were leaving.

NINE

I rolled past the tents of the poor folks waiting for something better to come. They studied me like pale memorials, the dogs nipping at Jude Brown's heels. I had lost sight of Henry Stands but knew there was little road between here and Berwick for him to eat up without me. Yet I came to a meadow and saw no sight.

I pulled Jude Brown up slower as if walking a cemetery but I knew what was coming. Henry Stands was waiting at a defile in the trail with his horse as a shield. He did not have a loosed gun, which I took as politeness and deferment to our previous encounter, but he hailed me like a common roadman all the same.

'Stay where you are!' he hollered.

'It is me, Mister Stands!' I called. 'Thomas Walker!'

'You are to desist following me!'

I was not for turning. 'I am not following. I am walking the road.' I grew bolder. 'You do not own it.'

'The hell you know I don't!' He came out from behind his big horse. 'Go home, boy!'

'I am trying to!' I moved Jude Brown on.

He mumbled some grievance and lumbered toward and I braked up. I thought about getting down from my seat to meet him but then I would be conversing into his chest. Here we would be eye to eye. He came alongside.

'Are we to do this?'

'Do what?'

'Round and round like whatever this is! You to discommode me again and again!'

'I am merely going home.'

'Then go! I will not stop you. Let me see you go!'

I looked up the road. 'Are you not going along?'

'No.' He smiled at me and it was ugly. 'No. I am to stay here a smart piece! This is my favorite set in the whole world!'

'I am feeling tired myself, Mister Stands. I will go about the side of the road and rest awhile.'

He glared and wished to side-winder me, I am sure. 'Then I will go so you may rest the easier!' He stormed back to his horse and almost pulled it over with his weight as he went up. He looked back at me once and set off.

He would strain his neck the way he kept turning it on me. I let him go and then cracked on. We came against each other again down the road. The same as before. Him waiting for me.

'I can hear you coming like a railroad. That cart of

60

yours squawks louder than you do! I thought you were to rest?'

'A moment's respite is like a winter to me.'

He came at me again. 'I will tie you to a tree!'

'You will not!' But he grabbed me and hoisted me off like a sack of flour. 'You will not leave me to starve!'

He dragged me. 'Someone will be along soon enough.'

'And I will tell them to take me back to Milton. And I will tell Mister Baker that Henry Stands tied me to a tree and left me to nature!'

He stalled. 'What manner of boy are you?'

'A good one if you would but know it!'

He shook me free and paced around, looking at the jury of the trees and mumbling curses. He had unhappily decided.

'If I am damned to be with company it will be on my terms and you will stand up to it.'

He did not give me the grace of concede or question but went straight for my wagon.

'I will work on how far and how long I am to take you, but it will not be with this carryall of yours.' He clumsily worked out the way that Jude Brown was hitched and I guessed that such sophistication was new to him. I protested but he would have none of it. He bounced the body up and down and the springs complained all around the trees.

'It is slow,' he declared. 'It has wood for iron. It will break and you will cry for your mother.'

He did not know what he said, I am sure. This wagon was bought when my mother gained color. It was true it was more to promenade than transport and was sprung for city streets, but it had been hers. She had ridden in it.

'I cannot leave it here!' My voice went high and I hated myself for it.

'Can *you* ride and will *he* ride?' He jerked a thumb at Jude Brown.

'Father used to ride him on his business sometimes.'

'Good. You will have no saddle and I know that will not suit you.'

'I do not mind.'

'You will tomorrow.' He had freed Jude Brown, who was happy for it and trotted over to the big black stud and nuzzled him as cats do. The stud ignored him.

He pulled out my sack from the wagon. 'What is this?'

'It is my food.'

'Well, that's a blessing. It figures you would not have any means to cook it up.'

'Thomas Heywood took our pot.'

'What a grand rogue this man must be.' He pulled the wooden Paterson out. 'And what the hell is this?'

'It is what it is. It is a model of the gun.'

He cocked and fired it. 'This gets better and better. Do you have wooden shot for it also?'

'As it happens there were but—'

'The great and terrible Thomas Heywood took thems as well?'

I nodded.

'Let us hope he thinks them ball-candy.' He dropped it back into the bag and walked to the horses, shoving the sack to me. He had done with the wagon. 'Pick up them reins. I'll tie you a blanket at least.'

I did and followed. He made a surcingle with the wagon's leather and with skill he tied the blanket to Jude

Brown and cut a short rein with a huge knife hilted with antler bone.

'Get up,' he commanded.

I surmised the situation without trying. 'I cannot. I will need a stump.'

He hauled me up by my pants. 'Gets better and better,' he growled, and set me on Jude Brown. He led off and I traipsed after. I looked back at the Brewster.

One of the most melancholy sights in the world is a forlorn wagon. I am told that they litter the plains. The skeletons of settlers' hopes and dreams. Piece by piece I was losing what little I had and getting closer to the little I had in front of me.

I imagined a carnival tent with a man in a red coat and top hat lording over my wares.

'See here! These are Thomas Walker's father's bones. Left out in the wild by an ungrateful son with blankets to keep him warm! These are his clothes and this pile of iron is the guns, kettle, and pot he let be taken from him, and the last pistol entrusted he gave away in his selfishness. And finally, this sad, sorrowful object is the wagon that his mother loved. Left on the side of the road like carrion.' After a pause to let the crowd shake their heads he would raise his arms. 'But, folks, that is not the worse of it. Behind this curtain is Thomas Walker's greatest villainy, the final insult and his greatest shame.' But he would not reveal it for free and I did not have the extra ten cents to see it yet.

We went on in silence with me behind, watching Henry Stands's and his horse's haunches roll lazily side to side. It would now be close to dinnertime, judged by my belly-growl, and I knew that the next settlement along our path would be Bloom's. I asked if we would be stopping to eat.

'You will eat in the saddle. We will stop before dark.'

Like most civilized folks', my belly was used to a large dinner and a simple supper. All this dry-food nonsense of sea-tack and jerky was for crows. Besides, the movement on the road did not play well with my water.

'I will have to stop for a moment,' I called.

'I will not,' he called back without moving his head, but I think he slowed anyways.

I got down for my business and with difficulty held Jude Brown's reins in my hand while he looked and huffed at me and did his business just where he stood to show how foolish I was to not be able to do the same. After I was done I went through my bag for some dodgers to chew on the road and stuffed my pockets, now envious of Henry Stands's jerky.

It was at this moment that I realized I could not get back on Jude Brown! With no saddle horn or stirrups for purchase I was like a mouse to a lion. I tried but every time I scrambled Jude Brown tripped forward and I brushed off. Mister Stands had gone from sight now for the road was hilly. I settled down quickly and led Jude Brown on. I would look for a log or a stump and if I walked quickly I could probably catch up. For the most part of the morning out of Milton we had gone across wide-open land, the blue mountains like another country on our right, but now we were in woodlands and had been climbing all the while. The ghost trees of winter had gone and everything was green but high up. You could see quite a way left and right through the narrow trunks but I kept my eye keen for a step so I could mount again. This was a very pretty time and even with all my woes I felt a peace about the nature of it all that you do not get in the city. To my surprise I came upon mister Stands as if waiting for me, a spyglass to his eye. He saw me approach and folded it and a leather packet of paper into his bags. Perhaps he had been pretending to look at a map and landmarks instead of holding for me!

He wheeled away before I could ask for a hand but soon enough I spied a dead log and pulled Jude Brown into the wood to jump on it. I was sure that mister Stands had accepted a level of responsibility to me, however reluctantly. I felt safe for the first time in a while and he let me catch up.

'I had almost forgotten about you,' he said over his shoulder, and I smiled because he could not see it.

TEN

The road climbed, the wind took up our coats, and the clouds fell about the hills, and I understood why Henry Stands wore a greatcoat in April. I did not recognize any of this country although this would have been the way I had come. I ached for conversation and for rest. My rear had become raw bone and I wondered when Bloom Town would show and reconcile me.

Eventually mister Stands raised his hand and turned off the trail. Without ask or tell I dismounted and went off for wood and stones. The unfortunate was that although I had my sofkee I had no means to cook it and I did not know how to word this comfortably with a man who hardly talked; anyhow, mister Stands did not like my wood.

'This is dead. And you are a deadhead traveling free

as you are. It will smoke and blind us both all night. Did your father not have an ax to cut?'

'We did just fine with fallen wood.'

He harrumphed, as he would, but made up the fire anyways. 'Go downhill until you find water.' He handed me his canteen after filling up his boiler, which was not much bigger than a can, and I missed my Dutch pot. I was thinking of my hunger, and that small boiler would have to cook twice to feed us both. I took our canteens and wandered down and down until I found a stream, which was full of leaf trash that sucked into the canteens more than the water and I picked them out constantly, which they seemed to find game as they did it again and again.

It was getting to twilight when I came back. I had fallen once and now had a little finger that I had landed on that hurt like I had broken my hand, but I would not tell it. Mister Stands had made his camp with the horses tethered and had boiled tea. He had a mug at least but I did not expect him to have another. He handed it to me to share and I took it with my shirt cuff pulled over my hand for it was boiling and he chuckled at this. It was strong as ever I had it and went all around me like a blanket and I forgot about the walk to the stream and back. I went to hand it over and said thanks.

'You drink it. I will have rum. Fill it up again and we will empty the boiler for your Indian meal.'

I was happy to do so. If he would eat my sofkee I would no longer be his deadhead. We would be partners.

He had laid out his oilcloth with bedroll on top and

sat on a log in a faded red capote shirt and braces and replaced his hat with a wool cap. He laid his belt with its guns and pockets beside him, his knife and ax on his blanket. He now looked like a riverman instead of the marauder previous. He had a great belly and broad limbs that looked like they could carry anything he cared to. I had never seen a bigger man, not one of older age anyways. He looked larger with his coat off. The length of it slimmed him down.

'Do you take rum?' he asked. He pulled the cork and offered it to me first. I gathered this is what he took as society.

'I do not.'

'For your tea. It will keep you warm.'

I accepted because these were the kindest words he had yet said. I tasted my new tea and did not regret it and he saw and nodded approval. He had dragged us two logs to sit on but I had no bed. I would sleep in my coat, I figured, or if that did not suit I could be a standee across the horses' rope. You had to pay for that privilege at a hostler if you could not afford a bed.

The tea gone, I filled the boiler again to make the sofkee and mister Stands filled a pipe. This was the first time I had seen anyone smoke. In the woods we were sheltered from the wind and as the lid on the boiler flapped with the heat I decided I would know more about Henry Stands.

'What is an Indiana ranger, sir?'

He rolled a little. 'You do not know?'

'It is something to do with the war?'

'The war! Ha!' He snorted and slugged his rum. 'There is a reluctance to call it what it was now our politic men

68

side with the English more than not. It was for independence again. Make no error.'

'What was your part?'

'To be a privateer. I wanted to sail but a ship is for a young man. I wanted to kill those blue-light traitors. But I was not for sailing. Before that, Tipton, that's John Shields Tipton, enlisted me in the rangers. I protected two forts with him and rode with Zachary Taylor, a Virginian like me, but that was in the Seventh Infantry. I believe they are both in Washington now. I was paid a dollar a day and had a smart leather hat and vest. We were militia and I believe we were smarter than those army buckskins. Could shoot at least. The shame of it came at Wildcat Creek. What them who were not there call the Spurs Defeat.' He spat and swallowed the words back with more rum.

'Thems who say the army turned and ran from the Indians with their spurs bleeding their mounts to gets away faster. Them scribblers call it the Spurs Defeat. That is true for some of the boys.' He drank longer. 'Not us.

'There was a man called Benoît who was a trader with the tribes. It was believed that he had betrayed what we would be at. He was caught and set to be burned alive at a stake. I took up my wind-rifle that I had taken from an Austrian fighting for the British and shot him before the flame was lit. No-one really minded. I just didn't see that any man should be killed like that. Just as long as he died was good enough.'

'And after the war? You were still a ranger?'

'We protected.'

'Protected what?'

'Settlers. Fought the Indians that had betrayed us in the wars. They started to move out anyways. I never killed one that did not go at me. Killed three Choctaw with my hands when they had pulled me from my horse. They were not much older than you. I have not now been a ranger for seventeen years.' He drank to this.

'What is your work now?' The rum had loosed his tongue and I had the conversation that was as good as food to me for without it my mind hung too much on what had passed. And I needed the words of men.

'Well, it may surprise that I was born in a brick house in Orange county, Virginia. My father had twenty slaves. I am an educated man and my father had served with Washington, and that's a fact you can bank. I had seven brothers and sisters. My father's name was Fear Stands— you may picture him from that. I know none of them now. I left when my mother died and took my inheritance before my father died on the agreement that I would not bother him again. I was a hell-raiser and dabbler in the flesh, which did not suit my rearing. In naught-eight I joined the Seventh and we went into Indiana and I met Tipton and he brought me into the rangers, who drank more and was looser, and that I liked.'

I had asked about his living and perhaps he had not heard me or perhaps this was his way of explaining it. He took a drink and got to it.

'I will sell tobacco and I will sell horses or anything I can. I do not want for much. You have caught me on my way to Cherry Hill, where they will have men who have escaped. Men like prison in the winter but the summer is not to their liking. You can live rough, you

70

can find work, find a crew and stay the hangman, impregnate a woman and plead her belly. They will pay me fifty dollars to bring one back.'

I jumped on his words. 'Perhaps this Thomas Heywood is one who has escaped!'

'That is as like. More he is a teamster on hard times. It is sorrowful for young men nowadays.'

I did not like these words of sympathy for a murderer. But I was all in with Henry Stands so I let it ride. He might have still kicked me to the road. The night came in and our Indian meal was done. We had one wooden spoon so eating was slow, but as it was hot I did not mind. He pulled out a yellow pocket map while I ate my share.

'Now,' he said. 'Let us see where to lose you.' He leaned back and forward at the map, squinting all the while. 'I have had this atlas yet two months and it blurs already. Damn their ink!' It was a small Tanner's atlas that showed the canals, railroads and stage roads of Pennsylvania and beyond. 'Well, we could go south to Danville—there will be law there—and report this matter to them. They would have a care of you. That is still Columbia county so they will take interest and you will be off my spine.'

This did not suit me and I was relieved at his next words.

'But that is off my path. So Berwick is here tomorrow and cross into . . . damn this ink! I know where I am going! Damn this ink! What is that? It is Luzerne but I do not know what!'

I came behind his shoulder and leaned over beside his ear. He smelled of smoke and firewood. I have never

71

lit a fire since and not pictured him nor seen a scarecrow and not smiled upon it.

The Tanner's atlas was colorful and exact. The greens and yellows like a mythical land. Lake Erie a monster in the left corner eating its way across. The fire did not help Henry Stands's eyes, nor the rum, I supposed. I pushed my head in closer. He snatched the paper away.

'I think you will not appraise! Eat your supper, deadhead.'

'I have young eyes. I can help.'

'And I am old, is it? Perhaps you can fetch me a cane and I will turn it to a switch! Sit down, boy.'

I went to my sack and with some slow thought took out my father's spectacles. Father had need of them for all time and he read his newspaper with them comfortably. I turned and offered them out for mister Stands.

'You may have lend of them. As to the map, I would not know what I am looking at to help you. Although why I should aid one so set on abandoning me I do not know.'

He rolled again and grunted, taking the spectacles and putting them on as awkwardly as fixing a blindfold with his fat fingers. He looked at the map with his new eyes and said nothing but I could tell he was satisfied. I went back to my eating. He looked gentler now, as if wearing a kindly mask. My father's face. He went over the map but he told me no more of his plans. When he was done he took off the glasses with care and handed them back without thanks. I folded them and put them in my shirt pocket.

I ate and finished my laced tea as the owls came out. Henry Stands would stop as one called out and waited for the other to reply, drinking some at each successful call.

I was drowsy with my tea and wanted to sleep but he bid me clean out the boiler before I fell and he watered the horses with his own canteen. This required him to tickle their throats up and he poured into them. He had to bite Jude Brown's ear to make him do this. His own horse was used to it.

He came back to the fire with his head down and waved a hand for me to come in close.

'Take up the boiler,' he whispered. 'Make like you are eating from it and pass me your cup.'

I was afraid at his low voice. This was the worst secret and I could feel it. I could see Thomas Heywood all around me. Mister Stands gave me a hard look. He was warning me to be still and his voice went on as if I would understand.

'An owl did not answer. Make like you are eating and give me that cup.' I shook as I handed it over and he looked at me as if I were dead. I ate my empty spoon and he poked at the fire.

'You see a white beehive over my shoulder in the trees?'

I put the boiler to my mouth as if draining it and studied the tree line. There was a white moon shape with stripes like a hive twenty feet away over mister Stands's head. It had twigs about it and was halfway up a tree. It blinked and I became hollow. *A face without!* I knew then that it was painted white and striped.

'We are not alone.' Henry Stands's eyes never raised from the fire. 'Drink your cup. There is another to your right. He has half a face.'

I did not know what this meant. I had to speak but kept it in the boiler.

'What is it?'

'Indians,' he said, and drew on his pipe.

There were no Indians in Pennsylvania. I as a boy knew that. Not for nearly a hundred years since Royal Proclamation and Teedyuscung. But my grandfather and Henry Stands's father had torn up British paper too. We followed the rivers and valleys that still had their Indian names. Mister Stands saw my fear.

'They are just hungry, that's all. They are the worst of them. Thems that stayed or were kicked away and became civilized like your Thomas Heywood. It is good that you have your hat and coat. In the fire they may not see you as what you are.'

I was almost out of my body with fear but Henry Stands kept up our talk as if it was nothing. 'Tomorrow we will go to Berwick. You may consider if you want to go on.' He checked once to his gun belt, ax, and knife, and then gulped some rum and began to sing, tapping out a tune on his bottle, which you may know as a fife and drum for soldiers.

> 'Then to the east we bore away
> To win a name in story
> And there where dawns the sun of day
> There dawned our sun of glory
> The place in my sight
> When in the host assigned me
> I shared the glory of that fight
> Sweet girl I left behind me.'

He slugged again and chinked the bottle to the boiler in my hand.

'Is it gone?' It was the face over his shoulder that he meant. I spoke into the boiler at my lips.

'Yes, sir.' I did not know if this was good or bad.

'So has the other,' he said. 'I must check my rifle. Stay here.' He picked up his knife and went off into the dark to the horses. I sat and watched my hands trembling around the boiler in my grip, praying for his return. I thought of my home in New York, pictured the velvet curtains and the black-and-white-tiled hall. My mother's coffin in the parlor, when I could not help but grin at all the attention put upon me.

Henry Stands came back and sat down. 'No harm. The horse would let me know, but you can never tell. You should sleep now.'

Sleep? I could no more sleep than I could walk to the moon, but I made the pretense. It was only when I went to lie on the ground that Henry Stands noted I had no bed.

'God, boy! You are ill prepared!' He made me drink some rum. 'Keep your shoes on and take my roll and blanket. I will stay up. They may come back. They would have seen my guns.'

'You could bring your rifle here,' I suggested.

'Then they would know I had seen them. Now set down. You may sleep. I will sleep some in the morning when you will make me tea. Nothing will happen while I sit here.'

I lay down and watched him, the blanket about my face. He made a new pipe and had plenty of rum to see him through. I thought I had a dream of him cleaning his pistols and mumbling songs but I cannot tell that as true. I slept well with that giant sitting above and my father's glasses against my breast. A quilt about me in the shadow of the valley.

ELEVEN

At sunup I used the last of the canteens for tea for I was not about to go down to the stream alone. Mister Stands was asleep but I guess he had kept his vigil for he had draped his kerchief across his eyes and lay on his coat deep gone. I still had cheese and crackers and I spread these on the sack for breakfast and hoped mister Stands would share some of his jerky. I tried not to stir him, but my striking a new fire for the tea jumped him awake. He growled and rolled over in his coat but he could not complain if I was making him food. I burned myself again and again striking the fire and making the tea; everything about tea is always red-hot despite its reward.

I put the mug near his face and he breathed it in. He sat up and drank it all and took my cheese and crackers without a word. He did not look like he enjoyed mornings but I put that down to the rum. He handed me the mug and I poured tea for myself.

'Get some more water,' he said. 'I will feed the horses and get us ready.'

I thought of asking him to come with me to the water but his face was not pleasant. I drank my tea carefully, as the enamel cup kept it hotter than anyone could stand, and then went off as told.

An hour gone and we were moving. I ached and was sore in the worst places but mentioning would get no favor and would probably go bad for me. I went on as carefully as I could. Mister Stands must have sensed my discomfort for he was positively human and sang to himself sometimes and called back to me with much conversation, which was a great distraction.

'My wind-rifle is from the empire of Austria,' he said without provocation. 'You see this pack?' He slapped a leather satchel on the flank of his horse. 'That is its accoutrements. They are its only problems, but no less fuss than powder once you gets used to it. The man I took it from was unable to have it worded to me how to operate—being dead—but I was lucky to have a forester in the Seventh who had been with Lewis's party. I take it that your schooling covers them boys? Anyways, Merry Lewis had him the selfsame gun. He demonstrated it to every Indian tribe they met. That man wrote a million words but he mentions that gun on page one. It was maybe twenty or thirty years old even then. Gunpowder ruins a gun. It is doomed the moment it is fired. You should tell your mister Colt about it.'

'How is it that it can fire so many shots?'

'You do not understand about air?'

'I do not.'

'I imagine your britches know better. The gun has a reservoir in the stock that I must pump. It is good for seventy shots, I have found. The first forty will kill anything. After that I am just winging and wearing down. Say now.' He pulled up and looked about. We were on open road at about ten in the morning. 'This looks like a spot. I will show you and let you show me. A boy should know how to fire a rifle.'

I now understood mister Chet Baker's words. Henry Stands liked to shoot. I suppose this habit had come from the war and his ranger life. What men make of themselves after violence leaves is up to them. I could only imagine what Henry Stands pictured when he shot at trees and rocks.

He unsheathed and drew out the gun. It was brass, wood, and steel and was clean with it. The leather stock was rounded and he explained that this was the reservoir for the air.

'Once empty it can take me an hour to fill it. She carries a load of twenty-two. Forty-six bore.' He pointed out a tube along the barrel. 'I can fire forty shots in about a minute.'

I knew that to be impossible. This was an old-man brag. He led me off the road into a meadow and scanned for a target.

'What you have to consider is that Lewis and Clark went across the land and did not get attacked once. Hundreds of tribes. And you gotta ask yourself why that was.' He scowled at me as if I was holding out the answer on him.

'Why?'

'Say you're an Indian. Say you've fought white men before. Seen armies of 'em. And what do you do before you attack?'

'I do not know.'

'You let them fire their single shot at you and then you swarm at 'em. But old Lewis there brings out his gun and right in front of them can rattle off a dozen shots without a break. That is the diplomacy of fire-power. But he made sure they never saw him empty the gun or load it up. To them it was without limit. Now, to them Indian minds, for all they know the whole party has these guns. There is no smoke, no reload, no powder, and there could be a million white men marching over the hills with this new medicine. They were afraid. And if you make a man afraid, you don't have to kill him. Remember that.' He put the gun in my hands.

'If you can put fear in a man you can beat him. It is not what you can do. It is what you might do that is the thing. No-one ever sees a man standing on his pile of the dead. He does not carry his destruction with him. Now take a set.'

I knelt and pushed the fat stock into my shoulder. It was not as heavy as I had thought. He bid me to find my mark and I set on a boulder the size of a bull.

'It has a ball in the chamber. Cock it one hand. One hand, mind, or I'll take it from you. Hold your other hand as far along as you can, stiff as feels right, and she will steady.'

'Who made this?'

'An Italian. All Italians are genius. There is a man in Philadelphia who makes them also but only for sport or fancy. This is a soldier's gun. Stop your breathing and take your shot. There will be no spark so don't flinch your eye.'

I held my lungs and fired. There was the crack and a lesser kick and smoke blew off the boulder across the field, fifty yards away.

I did something magical!

Too few times in a person's life does something wondrous occur but it is the sharing of the experience that elevates it. Henry Stands saw it in my grinning face and there was nothing in the years between us. He had done this once for the first time also. I forgot my troubles for a moment.

'Good,' he said. 'See that lever in front of the hammer? You push that to the right and hold the gun up just enough and you'll feel a new shot roll down.'

I did so, and other than the roll and set of the ball this was a silent action.

'Now it is ready to be cocked and fired again. Go on. You can kill that rock no more.'

I shot again and was rewarded with another puff of stone.

'How is it that men do not use these all the time?' I marveled.

'Well, it is not perfect. And powder is an industry. There is no profit in air. Its worse attribute is that the pump must be used often to shoot again.'

'But you could stop an army before that!'

He took the rifle and stroked my fingerprints from it.

'I heard said that Napoleon made it death to own one. He was fearful that there might be an army with 'em.'

I stood up. 'It is as you said.'

'How is that?'

'Put fear in a man.'

'Now you know how no Indian went for Merry Lewis. Shame he killed himself. Real shame.'

This was a dark end to our talk and we went back to the horses in silence. We rode on but there was no attempt by mister Stands to distance himself from me. I was alongside him when Bloom Town appeared below us, and I guess that street looked up right curious at two partners riding in with the sun at their backs.

Henry Stands had a lot of tricks learned from the road. He paid a mother in a log house a pistareen to use her grease and stove and cooked up some belly slices and beans he had bought from mister Baker. She gave us soda bread for free and a plate each and we sat outside on her porch to eat. Mister Stands shared but grumbled about the bill I was gathering.

'There will be a reckoning according on this, dead-head,' he declared.

The mother had three children who ran around almost naked.

'Why don't you play with them awhile,' he said. 'I could do with not looking at your face in front of me for a spell.'

'They are babies. I do not like children all that much.'

'You are a baby. And I do not like children, yet here you are.'

I did not like his proclivity. 'Do you not have family? No wife?'

'I do not.' He ate angrily. 'I am past liking women. I do not like their talk.'

'Why not?'

'You meet a woman and you will strive to fit. *I will do this, I will do that,* you say. And what do they say? I will tell you. *He will do this, he will do that.* To hell with them. *You drink too much, you smoke too much.* All the things they forget that you did when you met them. They do not complain if you work too much, that I note. But you will have twenty years to learn this between grass and hay. It will do no good to you now. You will wake up one morning and be mad like all of 'em.'

I thought about my mother and father. I am sure they were happy in marriage and a preacher may tell me that they were now happy together. But they seemed very far away to me then. I would change subject.

'What plans do you have for me?'

His dinner finished, he rubbed his hands together and sifted the crumbs and grease from his whiskers. 'Fetch my atlas from my bags.'

I went to his horse, who eyed me with a snort. Jude Brown was loved up to him and no longer paid particular attention to me. I suppose that younger animals may see a patriarch in one older than themselves as puppies do to dogs, family or not.

I opened the leather bag as the tail swished at me and I whisted him still. I did not locate the Tanner's atlas at first, forgetting how small it was, and so moved out the leather notebook thinking it might have shifted between. I opened it with no intention. I opened it and had my judgment changed.

There, on cartridge paper after cartridge paper, were drawings of birds! Black-and-white and colored etchings

83

of dozens of birds! Special detail paid to their heads and beaks, for sometimes that was all there was, and even a white spot of light shaded carefully on their eyes. All of them looking up or to each other, some half-finished where they had flown too soon, their feet imagined, some singing silently.

The charcoal and pencil should have been crude with the fat fingers that must have struggled on them, but they were as delicate as the figurines one finds on blue porcelain. They sat in no trees nor indeed with any landscape. That was not important, clearly, for their likeness. I did not know what the importance was, and I turned openmouthed when his voice growled behind me.

'What are you about in my business?'

'I was looking for the atlas.'

He plucked the book gently from me. 'You have yet to find it.'

I was dumb. His face was sullen. I had been discovered in someone else's bed. I could only say the truth as it came to me.

'I like your drawings.'

'Are you mocking me, boy?'

'No, sir.'

He leafed through the pages and the anger dissipated from his features like water from a lock. 'How do you like them? You think me foolish minded?'

'No, sir. They are very good. But I do not know them.' I stuck a finger on a page and gulped. 'What is this one?'

He squinted for a moment and spoke quietly. 'That is a bluestocking. An avocet. He will see you before you will see him.'

I ran with my success. 'And his neighbor?'

'That is a chickadee. Do you not go outside?'

'I do not know birds.'

He slapped the book shut and put it back. He was mad. I had seen a naked side of him. 'Well,' he said. 'You should know something about them. You may think them God's decoration.' He rummaged for his map. 'But for fact there is naught so mean as birds.' He tightened his belongings away from my eyes.

'Birds will fight all day. Kill each other's young for a nest and eat them. There are empty nests each year. All the world is their enemy. Especially each other. I seen three pigeons take down a red hawk once. They whirled him round until he drowned in the air.' He pulled me away to the log house, with the map in his hand. 'They are worse than men.'

We sat down again and he spread the map on his knee. I was loath to talk. There was a bad silence emanating from Henry Stands's form. I had not meant to do him wrong and I did not think he should be shamed for having a liking for something beautiful. I felt bad for him and myself. I had ruined the first good morning. My shooting lesson long gone.

I think he thought that I now felt less on him when I would have told any man that I did not think he cared a stick for any of my thoughts.

I shuffled my feet at his as he studied the map with difficulty and found myself holding out the folded spectacles again.

'What's this?'

'For your reading,' I mumbled, sorry as I could, my head down.

85

He took them and checked once that no-one saw and put them on. 'Much obliged.'

I scuffed my shoes in the dust. 'You can keep them. If you want.'

'No, that's fine.' He did not look up.

'They are worth four dollars anywhere. They will pay for me to no longer be your deadhead.' I turned so he would not see my red face. 'You may draw even better with them.'

I walked back to Jude Brown and went around him. I made that I was tightening the straps for the blanket so Henry Stands would not see me cry, my head behind my horse.

I heard him coming and I wiped my face on my coat and made more noise with the straps. He went up on his stud and looked down at me. He had put away the spectacles.

'I think that woman has taken a fancy to me, which is time to go. I aim to make Berwick before sundown. You better go to her stoop for a leg up. Or take my hand now.' He held it down to me and I did not mind that he saw my mottled face. I took his fist and he swung me up. He looked about. 'I think that there are too many Bibles around these parts for men like us.'

We both waved our hats at the mother and her brood, and we went off east again.

TWELVE

We made Berwick before dark. This was a canal town proficient in lumber and coal and you will recall that I stayed here when my adventure held promise.

It was welcome to see. I feel for those canal towns now. The railroad took from them their importance and we lost the pleasure of being pulled by six stout horses along a towpath. People pleasure-cruised in those days and Berwick was right popular for it. You took a picnic and a day and went through mountains and shared food at the locks with settlers. The canals made friends of strangers. Then the railroad came and people got in a right big hurry. What was at first a means to get the anthracite and wood into New Jersey became a passenger service. I will never understand why folks wanted the smell and the jarring back of the railroad over the tranquillity and beauty of the canals. People do not know when they have it good. I will show you a man who works on the river and a man who works on the rail and we will see who smiles more and lives longest.

Now we would have to cross the Susquehanna, which had been our partner. Into Luzerne and Nescopeck just across. The Delaware gap was a couple of days away now and the water reminded that I was near to home. But this was a proper town and though good and religious it was a town with story buildings, and Henry Stands was a man and I was worried that a saloon or coffeehouse confectionary would be his order. As I said before, they were still making reparation to the bridge, so it would be a punt across to Nescopeck and our road, but that would be in the morning. I spoke out that my father and I had slept here in a good hotel but mister Stands did not respond. He pulled up and looked about.

'I do not like to socialize,' he said. 'This place has changed a lot in two years. They most as like have a rule about camping. But I'm not one to pay for lodging. Yet we cannot ride through without a raft.' He wheeled his horse and studied the good folks. 'Lot of proper hats and suits. Too many Bibles. I am a Proverbs man only.'

I guessed he was wary of this society. Although he would not like New York, I am sure he had more kinship with the gangs of the Bowery and its points than he would care to admit.

'We could stay at the hostler,' I suggested. I was relieved that he would not seek company and drink. I had come to suspect that beyond the birds of his study, who could not converse, Henry Stands disliked the clamor of men. I knew blindly that this was not in fear of them. His father's name was Fear, he had told. I reckon that was as far as its meaning went to him.

'Aye, that might do.' He let me lead the way.

The hostler was a drunken man in apron and stained shirt. His only mark of decency was a well-groomed mustache. He shrank at the large body of Henry Stands and was meek in his presence.

You must take in that Henry Stands cut an imposing manner: he was the 'full-team,' as people say.

There were the guns that always hovered about his wrists from his waist and poked out of opened holsters and that he rested on as he waited for a returned word. I imagined he kept this posture be you judge or street hawker. There was the greatcoat and cavalry leggings and old hat that reeked of a life already past yours. He entered every room and space with a check around like he owned it and did not care if you were there. He carried his horse behind, a black war-horse, bred from Spanish, that befitted the man, and the hostler gave us a cent rate to sleep there, and Henry Stands's stance made clear that he was doing him a favor by sparing him. I was squire to his knight and no-one questioned my presence. I was man by his proxy and tried to carry my own bearing as if I had inherited his power.

'We'll fire out the back for our meal,' he told the hostler, and there was no question otherwise. 'I will not pay for your water and will not charge you for watching your horses.' He joked but the hostler thanked him instead of laughing and made himself scarce.

Plenty of water was welcome; we filled the horses and our canteens and boiled tea and sofkee without a care to wasting.

We sat on hay-bales in the dark in the hostler's yard and Henry Stands poured a circle of water around the fire for safety and seemed gentler when he replaced his old hat for his wool cap. The tea shrank and changed to rum and I began to find it sweet. I had sneaked gin and did not care for it but rum I found was like liquorice and sugar, if you took it careful, and it did not burn like whiskey. We talked about my road. Henry Stands suggested that at Stroud we would split. It was a town with law and marshals but out of Columbia, being Monroe, but they would spread word back on my behalf. Danville would be interested in Thomas Heywood, the good Chet Baker my witness. A stage road could take me the rest of the way and mister Stands could continue on to Cherry Hill. I said that I had no money for a stage.

'Presbyterians will care for you. You must understand that I must be about my business.' He sucked on his spoon. 'From Stroud you can get to the Delaware gap. That is where you came in, is it not? Canals and proper roads to take you home.'

'I understand that you wish to abandon me. That is fair enough. So far we have been travelers along the same road, that is all.'

'That it is.' He gave the spoon to me.

'And it has not been my wish to burden you.'

'You have not.'

I began to well up again but fortunately it started to rain, a full rain, and we concentrated on that and moved ourselves to the barn to look out from the door, the spoon back in the boiler, and it rattled with the fall.

I did not want to leave him or have him leave me. I wanted to be home and safe. I did not see that possibility without him and if I were a man as I am now I may have known the right words to say. As it was he watched the rain falling and pooling in the yard and said nothing. I grasped at straws. Thin words that I hoped would stick.

'I would not be able to pay you unless we reach Paterson.'

'Never mind.'

I had to raise my voice above the rain, which was drumming the barn. 'Mister Colt will pay for my father's orders. Near seventy-five dollars. I will have no further business with him. You could have it all.'

'That is all right. You will need it.'

This was without hope. If Henry Stands did not want coin, I had nothing. I was a boy so why not be a boy instead of whatever I was pretending to be? I had a right to cry. There was no-one to admonish me anymore. I was the dirty clothes on my back and a horse and a wooden gun.

'Why do you not *help* me?' I rubbed away my tears, hateful for myself, but damn if I could not stop. I was worse than the rain. '*Why* do you not understand? I am afraid! I do not know where I am! I only want to go home and I want you to take me there . . . and I will pay . . . my aunt might like you . . . I do what I am told . . . I am trying to be good for you, yet you . . .'

I turned away. I would rub Jude Brown until I stopped crying. Henry Stands did not warrant my shame.

He kept his back to me. There were several horses in the barn and they steamed now as the damp air came in. They all eyed me solemnly and then enviously as I stroked Jude Brown and felt the knots in his muscles.

I was sniffling down my face but did not mind. I had the time for it now and had delayed it too long. It felt good and I still do not understand why that was so. Sometimes you just have to cry and sleep better for it.

Henry Stands's head went below his shoulders. He took his half bottle of rum from his coat pocket and drank and watched the rain. He swigged and paid me no mind and watched our fire drown. After a time, when Jude Brown's eyes began to droop with my strokes, Henry Stands spoke out into the night, not turning to me.

'Thomas Heywood, you said?'

'Yes.' I stopped my strokes and my tears.

'Thomas Heywood. Did Chet know that or did you?'

'Both. There was a meeting at mister Baker's the day before.' I coughed out my next words. 'With my father.'

He drank long and took off his cap to wipe his brow. The rain made his hair quite thin and I now noticed he was gray.

'So this thief and murderer knows your name?'

I had not thought on this. I can still feel the coldness on my skin. The flesh at my wrists pimples as I write.

'Yes,' I said. 'He would.'

'Then he would mostly like to correct the error of letting you go. I suppose he has sobered up and thought on it. As I would have done.' He came back into the barn. 'That changes some things.'

'What things?'

'Well, he may have assumed you are back to home. He may be setting to clear his writs. Milton would not be a place for him now. He may run west. That is what I would do. But Chet said he is a workingman, such as that is nowadays, so being an outlaw may not be his chosen. He will most likely sell your father's guns for a month of drink. But there is a trail. There is you, for one. You will report the crime. You will report the murder. But only if you are alive.'

'You think he may be after me?'

'That is an assumption. I would care that you do not judge me on my next line.'

He fixed me with his stare and rested on his hip as I had seen Thomas Heywood do.

'I would be. If he were me. *I* would be after you.'

I came out from around Jude Brown. 'What am I to do?' My tears had started again.

'Well, we need to get you under the cover of law. That is assured. We are on the road east. Directly as you came. He may have come across your Brewster by now. How many you say is with him?'

'Three more.'

'I should have gone to Danville. Between now and Stroud is swamp and mountains. I should leave you here. That would be the thing to do.'

I ran at him and wrapped myself around his waist, his belly on my chin, and the smell of smoke and damp surrounded as his coat fell about me.

'*Don't!*' I choked out. 'Take me home! I want to go home! Don't let him get me!'

His hands did not close on me when that was all I needed for the night. He stiffened and held me away.

'This is not for me. You need the law and that is it. I am not . . . I am on my own.'

I pulled away. I was getting used to wiping my eyes with my cuff.

'You have a gun that can kill twenty! You boasted an infantry and have guns aplenty! What are you afraid of? I am asking you for help! Perhaps you prefer birds to your own kind!'

A blank opened between us. The only sound was the rain on the roof and I took my cause further.

'You say you were born in a brick house yet we are in a barn! You stand in people's doors and pay for their grease rather than sit in a proper eating house! You have no work and want to beg to hunt men from Cherry Hill. I have a contract that will pay and I *do* live in a brick house with a tiled floor and parlor and an aunt who would look for a husband to protect her if you would care!'

I stomped the straw.

'Indiana ranger! I do not know what that is, but now I will never know, I'm sure. And when I get home I will read up on your war and write something on it myself and about those cowards who were in it!' I steamed around, kicking straw.

'You would leave me to die when I have asked for your help and will pay!' I stopped my stomp. 'I know I am before my age. That is because I can read and grew up in a city and my father and mother taught me to be. But I know that my father would walk up to a door of a person he never met and would sell them his wares when they did not want. And he was bold enough to take mister Colt's guns on an unknown road into unknown territory and that makes him bolder than you, Henry Stands! And he had no gun and stood up to four men and died because of it!'

I expected the side-winder slap and tried to take it well but I flew on my back. I was light for my age.

I rolled up and watched him pour out his boiler into the rain and pack it on his horse. I rubbed my burning face where he had struck me and watched as he kicked open the outer doors and led his horse out into the rain.

He looked up the road where we had come and then to the new one, the rain misting off him. He went round in a circle, judging both roads, his horse feeling the ground, and then he whipped the reins and sped off into the night, east.

He was gone, without looking at me further since the moment he hit me. I did not know that adults would leave children, but Henry Stands was a bad one, I now knew.

I shut the doors and went to my sack. I took the wooden Paterson and slept in an empty bay on my coat, warm in the straw, and the gun with its sweet smell of oil at my chin. I was empty of tears and as I said, and as you know, you may sleep better for it.

In my sleep I saw Thomas Heywood stalking me in the rain and the dark. The rain covering his footsteps like he floated above the road, and me now alone with a wooden gun. I saw faces covered in brown scales, their eyelids just pus. And I dreamed of horses. Mostly of the sound of them coming back or chasing me. But it was only dreams.

THIRTEEN

I was kicked awake by the hostler in the morning. Although it was before noon he was already harsh-breathing with drink. I dragged myself back to the wall and rubbed my rump where his boot had met me.

'What are you about here?' he demanded. I gathered he had forgotten in his drunkenness that we had paid for the night or had grown confident now that he could not see a big black horse and the man to go with it. He had some pride to take back and I guessed kicking a boy would do it; such is the way with trash.

I stood up. 'I am here with my horse, if you will remember.'

'What about your old man?'

'He is a drinker and has gone. And he is not my father if that is what you mean.'

'Then you get out of here. Out with you.' He shooed me with flapping hands like I was a turkey and I looked at him as if he was soft-headed. I took up my things and led Jude Brown out of there.

The road was muddy from the night and already coated my laces. I looked up the road and spoke to Jude Brown like he was human.

'Come on, Jude. We will breakfast on the road.'

I talked to him all through the town as we slopped slowly and drew strange looks but Jude seemed to take comfort from it and so did I. Animals are good like that. I have to this day always had a dog and a horse and do not trust people who do not care for either and I will give no time to a man who beats either. In fact I will give him less and with my right hand and foot if I sees him beat down on one. Until you have had a horse breathing beside your ear, eating from your hand, stepping with your step, and thanking you with his head nudging against you, the Lord is your stranger.

My path was cut by three ladies in black dress and bonnets. They were plain or old with faces like my aunt's and had watery eyes when they looked at me. I guessed I must have looked mighty dirty and red-faced, which happens when you are hungry, for they took pity on me instantly.

'Sakes, child.' The oldest of them stopped me. 'Where are you going?'

I told them the truth, for the question was straight enough. 'I am to Paterson, New Jersey, and then on to New York.'

'*New York?*' I might have said to Paris the way she exclaimed. 'Why, child? Where is your family?'

97

They were holding my arms and shoulders now with their chalk hands. 'I have only my aunt, ma'am. I have a home in New York.'

'But where is your father and mother?'

'They are dead, ma'am. I am working back on my own.' I tipped my hat and tried to walk on but they still had words and stood in front of me.

'What is your name, child?'

'Thomas Walker, ma'am.'

'You are out here on your own, Thomas?' They all shared one head and shook them and looked me up and down.

'My father was killed days ago.' These words had become easier although I noted my tongue had become common, which is what happens when you hang with Hoosiers. My next had a lower tone. 'I am going home.'

The oldest clutched her chest. 'My, my! Have you made report of this, child?'

'I will, ma'am. I will get to Stroud and do that.' I tried to move on but they blocked me again.

'You are a brave boy, praise the Lord! But you will need a bath and proper food. Eggs and bacon. Come with me, child.'

Now you can judge me how you will, and I know Presbyterian women when I see them, but after my night of abandonment a hot wash and some eggs and bacon was a prospect better than a gold mine to me then. I could do with a little bit of dependence. They laid their hands on me and escorted me and Jude Brown away.

*

I was taken to one of their houses, a three-story white wooden house on the edge of the town with trees and rocks in the garden and a proper fence.

An ancient black man grinned and raised his hat at me and gently took Jude's rein from my hand with just two fingers. He led Jude to the rear of the house and that horse never even looked back at me.

The older of the women thanked her friends but told them to hurry on to church and to excuse her on her behalf. I realized then that it must be Sunday. I had lost all sense of the days. I took my hat off without being asked and she smiled at me, which was like a fold in an old shoe.

She seemed intent on dragging me up the stairs, which I did not care for. I was not a baby reluctant to bathe, and I politely wrung my hand back.

She pulled up her black skirts to her ankles as she stomped up the stairs and called out to the whole house as I followed.

'Martha! Abby! Make a bath!'

I saw two girls in white peer up at me through the balustrade from below as if I were a ghost they had only just seen.

I was taken to a bedroom and told to undress and she left me, but only for a moment, to bring me a fresh-laundered smock of sorts. I was hesitant to undress in front of her but she told me she had three sons and not to be so foolish. I put up my sack to the bed.

It was considered unhealthy to bathe totally then, of course, and in winter it was almost illegal in some towns, a sign of madness. So I was stood in the kitchen in a wooden tub while a black girl in ribboned pigtails and josie dress poured stove-warmed water over my head. I had twigs and bugs on me that I never knew!

Water was quite a commodity in those days, sold door to door, but they did not spare it, and judging by all the glass and tin and cushions and rooms, this was a fine house.

I thought it only right that I should know the name of the person seeing me naked and washing my head.

'I'm Thomas,' I said.

'They call me Black Jenny,' she replied. She was only a couple of years older than me but I guess the old lady thought I could not be shamed in front of a black girl. She had cheap tin-framed half-lens glasses. I knew the price of most spectacles. I still judge some folks by them.

'Why?'

'Why what?' She stopped with the water and soap at last.

'Why do they call you Black Jenny?'

'Because there is a white Jenny.'

'Do they call her White Jenny?'

'No.' She passed me a towel and I hid my shame.

'Who is the lady?' I asked as I dried.

'That's Mrs Carteret. She wants to see you in the keeping room when you're dressed.'

My stomach still had plans. 'She said I was to eat?'

'I ain'ts feeding you!' She said this as if I had insulted her mother.

'What's a keeping room?' I had never heard this phrase.

'Are you dumb, boy?'

I reckon she must have meant the parlor. 'Where are my clothes?'

She handed me back the white smock. 'Your clothes are to wash. Why do you have a wooden gun? Ain't you too old for toys?'

I did not consider twelve too old for anything, but I was shocked that my sack had been burrowed through. We did not do such things in New York. I had come across Henry Stands's sketchbook accidentally and had at least apologized.

'It is not a *toy*,' I snapped. 'I doubt you have anything so fine.'

'It don't do nothing.' She crossed her arms and her spectacles flashed in the light so I could not see her eyes.

'It is important to me. That is what it does.'

I had done with talking to fools who did not recognize precious things. I pulled on the smock and, as I sat clearing my head, realized a white girl had taken Black Jenny's place. She did not acknowledge my surprise and put a plate of bread and headcheese into my hand.

'Sit at the table, boy,' she instructed.

I took my enamel plate and sat, disappointed at my fare. I did not eat pressed pig's feet and ears. I figured these girls were teasing me and I asked for some cheese and milk.

She grunted at me and went to a long cupboard. She was blond and very pretty and again a little older than me.

I was wise enough not to trust pretty girls. They will promise you a kiss if you close your eyes and then drop a spider down your shirt. Ugly girls will fight you but they do not laugh at your misfortunes that they have created such as pretty girls do. They will find a cowlick a disability and your britches will always be too short or too long and they will fun you.

She came back with a muslin-covered jug and paper-wrapped cheese and sat with me.

'What are you doing here, boy?' she asked as if she was in charge of the whole house. She had not brought me a glass for the milk and I settled that she was holding out on me until I answered her questions. I queried straight back.

'What are *you* doing here?'

'Mrs Carteret is my guardian. She looks after us girls here.'

'How many are you?'

'Five. My mother is a fallen woman.' She said this as if her mother were in debt to her. 'Mrs Carteret is making a lady of me.' She raised herself up and flicked her dazzling hair from her ear with a porcelain hand.

'Are you an orphan, boy? Is your parents dead?'

She was not shy. I bit off a lump of cheese and bread together in one bite so that I would be too polite to answer. She pushed away from the table and fetched me a glass.

'Be careful with that.' She smiled when she put it before me. 'It is very expensive. It came from a place called Holland. I think Mrs Carteret would have you whipped if you broke it.'

I was not a saphead for fooling. She had guessed me for a country boy. She was ruffled plenty when I poured the jug like I did not care if I broke the table.

'You are an insolence!' She sat back down and watched me eat. 'If you are an orphan, boy, you cannot stay here. This is a house for *girls*.'

'I do not wish to stay *here*. I have a house and an aunt. I am on the road with my own horse. I have stopped here for a wash and some food as was offered. I will be gone when my clothes are ready.'

'You are a liar! "House", indeed! With your clothes all stinking! Mister Markham will see through you!' She stuck her tongue out at me, which seemed real childish for all her pretenses.

'Who is Mister Markham?'

'See!' She leaned back and folded her arms again. 'You don't know nothing!'

'I know that if I do not know nothing, then I must almost know everything.'

She looked at me confounded and then reached across the table and pushed over my glass of milk.

'Now see what you did, boy! Mrs Carteret is going to make you safe to be hanged!'

I was done with children, as I was at home when I watched them from my windows fighting and throwing stones at each other or dancing with dogs.

I tidied up the glass and my wet smock with a cloth that I got myself. It was true I had cried lately and had relished it as a child might but I did not understand children's ways. No, that is not true. I understood them. I just hated them. Hated being them.

When I had gone along the road with my father and shot at imaginary Indians I had been quiet and felt guilty for enjoying it. Then I had seen my father killed and seen real Indians among the trees and been left by my only hope in the world. I did not entertain being a child ever again.

Mrs Carteret came in and the girl bounced to her side.

'He spilled his glass, Mrs Carteret!'

She told her to hush and not to mind. 'Now, Martha, he's just shy, that's all.' She held out her arm for me, her palm down. 'Come with me, Thomas. Come on, boy.'

I put down the cloth and went around the table. Mrs Carteret took my hand and Martha waited for Mrs Carteret to look aside and leaned in on me as I passed and kissed my cheek.

I never saw her again but I have never forgotten that sly peck, and I have forgotten hundreds of kisses. The sly ones are the best.

I have met many men since of the like that encompassed mister William Markham. They are those middle-aged, waist-spreading, no-neck types who have lost the joy and privilege of life with the loss of their hair. They have little control in the movings of the world but rule like kings over what little they do possess. I have found that they often use charities, churches, and government as good places to hide and rule; the real world would see them for what they are and they would starve. They have education and a pen and will write to you to tell you that you are dead and inform you that you are wrong when you try to correct them.

He was in black cloth and white collar and sat at Mrs Carteret's parlor table like on a throne. He pulled down his glasses—eight dollars' worth, I reckoned—and summed me up as a boy in a white smock.

I had gone a good hour without thinking about Henry Stands and I had thought my road home was now safe and assured without him. Mister Markham did not see that it was all so simple. He asked me my name, confirmed that I had eaten, and then began.

'Now, Thomas, as I understand it, Mrs Carteret informs me that you have recently become an unfortunate among us. That your poor father has been taken from you in murder and you are now an orphan in our town. Is that a truism, Thomas?' He eyed me as if I would lie about such a thing for some headcheese.

'I know I need the law, sir. My father was killed by a murderer named Thomas Heywood, but I have a home in New York and my aunt—her name is Mary Sample—will care for me. She lives in our house.'

He shuffled his chair to show me his shiny trousers. 'Well, can you tell me what has befallen you, Thomas, so I may have a record of it, so as we may help you, son?'

I gave it all, calmly as I could, but got flushed at times, and he saw this and was kind enough to let me cool down and he stayed his pen and asked Mrs Carteret for some water for me.

I told him all about the good Chet Baker, and the deceit of the Hoosier Henry Stands, not modifying anything about that villain's treatment of me, including his swipe to my face and abandonment. I also stressed voraciously that it was most probable that the murderer Thomas Heywood was now set to find me to clear his mistakes.

Mister Markham took this all down with a purse of his lips and shaking of his head at my tribulations. He set his pen down the moment I had finished. I do not think he could have raced his pen fast enough to write the half of it.

'Thomas.' He pulled his waistcoat to fit better. Fat as he was I would have advised he do without. 'You do know how important it is to tell the truth, now, don't you, son?'

'I do, sir.'

'Is this all the truth, Thomas?'

'It is, sir.'

'Where do you live, Thomas?'

'New York. The city, sir.'

'And what is your address?'

I froze, and he saw it and smiled wickedly.

I did not know my address!

Understand that I can take you there, even today. I could guide you to that four-story redbrick house with the four stone steps off a cobbled street as sure as I can show you my son's graves. But I was twelve then and did not know. I did not need to know. It was my home. I lived in New York. I realized on that rug that I did not know where mister Colt's factory was neither, other than I could probably get there from the ferry.

'I . . . I know where it is, sir, but . . . but I am schooled at home. I do not go out much. It is near the river and the piers. In Manhattan. We left from Pier 18. Just a left and straight down.'

I blurted out some names of stores and tradesmen I knew but I could see I might as well have spoke of canyons on the moon. Mrs Carteret put her hand on my shoulder and squeezed as mister Markham rubbed his chin.

'Thomas.' He sighed. 'I must look more into this. I shall write to the council in New York with your father's name and your aunt's and we shall try to help you. I will also write to Mister Chet Baker to confirm your story as best he is able and—'

I interrupted, which I never did when adults spoke.

'But you can ride to Mister Baker's in little more than a day! I will take you!'

He adjusted himself again. 'I will *write* to Mister Chet Baker to confirm. That will be the way of it, son.' No doubt it was his pen that kept him fat.

'In the meantime you must spend some days with the good folks at the orphan asylum in Philadelphia. Our church's affiliation. They will care for you until we can find your proper place or—should you be imaginative in your current distress—a new family for you.'

I ran to the table and he ducked from me as if I might strike him.

'No! I have a horse! I can find my own way home! I have seen a map! I crossed the Delaware gap with my father! The road leads there! Mister Colt owes me seventy-five dollars! I can get home!'

'Son, you have no *money* on you to get you home! It costs coin to cross the Delaware and fare to New York city! As it is we must sell your horse to pay for your transit and support at the asylum. You have admitted to being an orphan. We cannot permit you to ride the road alone now that we have taken you into our conscience. Your aunt will be made aware, if she exists at all, and in time we will settle the matter. You are better off than some. I assure you it would only be for a month or two once my letters are responded.'

Mrs Carteret hauled me back by my shoulders, hushing me all the while, but I had more.

'There is my book! It has Mister Colt's details and my

107

father's hand. Take me to Mister Colt! Jude Brown is my mother's horse! *He is mine!*'

Mister Markham brushed me off him although I had not come close.

'Son, we do not wish you *harm*. But nor do we fly to the corners of the earth on a child's whims!'

The corners of the earth?

'We wish only to protect you. All will occur in its good time. The asylum is the safest place for you if you truly believe that a man may be out for you. You are in the arms of the Lord and, through my strength and honor, under the protection of the law. I promise that I will write a letter as soon as you are safely secured in St John's.'

Mrs Carteret whispered to my ear, 'It is for the best, child. The Lord preserved you and sent you to me. Praise be.'

She almost cursed at the ringing of the bell above the door and left me in the room with mister Markham. He looked at me sympathetically but I could respond only with red.

'My horse cannot be sold, sir,' I said. 'I have already lost my mother's wagon. I am not an orphan as you know it. I have a home. I only want to go home. I am despairing that no-one is willing to assist me!'

Mister Markham was not listening. He was straining his concentration to the hall. My life had been penned into his notes. The asylum door was already closing. I imagined only a great stone edifice and a door like on a castle in picture books and maybe my image was not that wrong for all that. I listened to the mumbles in the hall with him.

Mrs Carteret was insisting on someone. Their voices were muffled and polite and then stress began to rise in her feminine inflection as women of her ilk do when trying to be forceful. I heard her squeal as her own door pushed her aside and I recognized the voice that had flung her wide.

'Move, harpy! I am coming in, damn you!'

It was Henry Stands! And he was right to call that damn woman a harpy who had spirited me away like a siren with promise of eggs and bacon.

The door of the parlor crashed and there was the long coat and old hat and the guns.

And a giant in mister Markham's sight filled the doorframe.

Mrs Carteret shadowed but Henry slammed the door on her. I could have told her that Henry Stands had no time for women, even in their own houses. I hoped there was a mister Carteret who would come to defend his old wife. He would get his jaw broke for his trouble and regret meeting her when Henry Stands was done.

Henry Stands gave me no eye and only looked mister Markham up and down and snorted derisively through his beard as I should have done when I judged him.

'This boy is with me,' he said. I could smell the rum on him. 'I have been bestowed by his father to take him home.'

'And who are you, sir, to barge in so into a Christian home?' mister Markham pushed himself up on his chair arms. A mouse before a bear.

'My name is Henry Stands.' He stiffened up right tall and so did I. 'I am obliged that you looked after the boy whilst I had business. We will move along now.' He took my hand and I squeezed it back until my nails bit.

Mister Markham smarmed in his seat. 'Oh! So you be the same Henry Stands who put that red mark on the boy's cheek? Who abandoned him last?'

'The very same.' He tipped his hat. 'Thank you for looking after the boy.'

'Are you a blood relative, Mister Stands?'

'I gets around.' He pulled me to leave but mister Markham had already written a sheaf of paper about me with his pen.

'I only ask, Mister Stands, because Thomas here is now the property of the St John's Orphan Asylum for Boys. We will ensure that his family is found, and safe passage for him back home. You may relinquish your responsibility to him.' He pulled his waistcoat over his shirt, showing above his pants. 'He is in my care. And I speak for the *law*.'

Henry Stands stood still as if he came to this house every day to collect his rent, and mister Markham shrank a little.

'The law you understand is the law of advantage.' Henry turned on him fully. 'I would spit that these boys in your "asylum" get a dollar a month to be looked after by your church. And you get half to see to it. You get them sewing or cutting wood and making plows to make them a trade, you say, and sell on their work for profit. Each boy you take in is cents in your pocket. So you will rush to get him back to his family, will you not, man who has not introduced himself to me?'

Mister Markham flushed and spouted as if to burst: 'I am a God-fearing man, sir! I work for a charity under God!'

Henry Stands pressed my hand and I looked at it grow white.

'I am a man, sir, who takes back prisoners who have absconded. I have spent a time walking those men back to jail. I have heard their stories about your asylums that set them on their way.'

Mister Markham's flush went away and he paled, his lips white with anger. 'That boy is under my protection and is a record of the law, sir!'

I had never seen Henry Stands draw a pistol in the short time I had known him. They were there, his pistols, as ornaments on the man, and in truth I had seen him hold only one of my father's Colts and his magnificent wind-rifle. To see him throw down, to hear the leather scabbard scrape, was fearful and final. He did not do this for show.

Henry Stands pulled on mister Markham and I guessed that for mister Markham this was the first occurrence of such a sight in his life for his eyes near outgrew his spectacles.

Henry Stands cocked his pistol.

'So protect him.'

You did not want to hear that voice.

Mister Markham shivered under the gun. His demeanor reduced from firebrand to corpse, his eyes wider than them eight-dollar frames. He put up his hands and it would shame me to describe the sound of his pleading whines.

Henry Stands put back his pistol. 'Stay sat,' he

said. He leaned to the door with me still in his other hand, mister Markham gone from his mind.

'Come, son,' he murmured.

Son, he had said! And I absorbed the word like sunlight in winter. He had still not used my name and until that point in our association he had only ever called me 'boy.'

I never asked him why he came back. I have pictured often that he went on up the road in the night, in the rain, and cursed me.

He had found shelter under trees and drank his rum and cursed me.

He ate his corn dodgers and jerky and cursed me.

And then, somewhere in the dawn, he had looked back along the road and cursed me louder and came back to get me. And cursed all the way.

He pulled back the door and Mrs Carteret stood on the stair with a shotgun and cocked it to us.

'Mister,' she said calmly as if the steel were a rolling pin. 'I don't know who you are but this is my house. I have girls here. If I shoot you I am in my right. Let the boy go. The Lord has him now, you Hoosier *trash*!'

I looked up at Henry Stands and he pulled me behind him but his eyes were fixed to Mrs Carteret.

'Ma'am.' His voice was cleaner than I had ever heard it. No rum-and-tobacco harshness. 'I have never shot a woman.'

I think me and Mrs Carteret expected more from him but I think Henry Stands thought that enough. She must have looked at his past down her shotgun's twin barrels pointed at his eyes and seen the same as mister Markham. This was not the first time he had

112

stared down a gun. She let the barrels point to the floor.

'You *swine!*' she hissed through her tears. 'God help that poor boy. God save him from Hoosiers!'

I tugged his sleeve and brought down his ear. I was still in my smock and naked beneath but I would want my things. Henry nodded and threw his look back to Mrs Carteret.

'The boy's book for his business. Bring it. And his clothes. I will fetch his horse.'

I pulled him down again and he began to hush me but I insisted.

He put his hand to his holster. 'And the wooden gun, ma'am.' I tugged him down again and Henry took off his hat when he rose.

'The boy says, "Please," ma'am.'

FOURTEEN

I changed from my smock behind Jude Brown on the ferry to Nescopeck, glad for the clean clothes that were just a bit still damp. I buttoned up and watched Henry Stands look out over the river and across the green waiting for us on the other side. He had on his long coat and had his back to me with his black horse at his shoulder. There was one man at the rope and another at the punt. They had drooping hats, slack jaws, and grins and were mindful to keep their hunched backs low in Henry Stands's presence but winked at me all the while.

Henry Stands's back lifted and fell in deep breaths as he took in the Susquehanna. I watched him and although I knew he had done me a great deed I felt further from him. You may know this. It is as when a neighbor does you a service that you do not expect or a stranger stands up on your behalf. It is almost an embarrassment. To a boy beholden to a strange man it is better to stay quiet than say too much thanks.

I remember once back home in New York waiting in line with my father at some store—the butcher's would be it for it was early morning and the smell of blood and sweet sawdust before breakfast made me want to be sick. My father sent me over the road to the drain and I stood there for a time feeling bad. People passed me, hundreds of them, all ignoring a boy on the curb looking like he had been kicked by a horse. Then a man in a white-striped jacket and boater stepped out of the herd and put his hand on my back.

'Are you all right, boy?' he said kindly. 'Do you need some help?'

My father called and waved and indicated that it was okay, somehow miming that I was with him. This man, about my father's age, raised his hat and mimed back that he understood by winking across and then the same down to me and he receded once more into the whirl of the crowd.

I had said nothing. But it occurs to me often that at that time that stranger had broken from his morning, from his purpose, to come to my aid. I did not need him but it is the offer of being willing to invest that matters. By coming to the curb he was submitting to enter my troubles and I may have had a heap of them, a *thousand* of brick that he was committing to. And to Henry Stands now I did not know how to say thanks enough. My voice was small. No man across the street

115

'You have your father's book. You know the details of the gun. I have fired the piece. You have that paper from a president. What one man can do another can do.' He rose up. 'Do you not think that we could sell those guns? You with your father's schooling and me with my honesty. What say you, son?'

I looked around to the trees for guidance and smiled weakly. 'I do want to get on. If we move off going east, will we not add time to our days, sir?'

'A little. It will mean entering the Shades of Death a bit more than when you came through the gap.'

'Shades of Death?' I am sure I was not alone in questioning such a locale.

'The Great Swamp. It is the place of the Wyoming massacre. You will find that when Indians triumph and kill white folks it is called a massacre. When whites accomplish the murder of Indians it is called a battle.

'I see it this way: if your Thomas Heywood is following— though I'm sure he is long drunk and given you up for dead—he will not take the high road. Between here and Stroud is hills and forest. If we go north a spell we will be on higher ground. See a man following us yesterday.' He strapped his horse's neck and began to move on. 'Besides, I need a drink and your Mister Markham may set his women on the road to find you and wed me.'

I had no choice other than to accept that Henry Stands was right. Thomas Heywood may have shrugged me off as dead. He may have laughed over a campfire with that Indian-hatband fool that it was shouting at the moon to go after a boy and a wooden gun. They would have drunk me away and tossed the empty bottles to smash on the trees.

But he might not have, and I was in danger still and that thought is enough for a boy without a roof over his head.

Henry Stands pulled up again. 'Show me that thing again.' Henry Stands held out a gloved hand. I rode with my sack at Jude Brown's neck, so I took out the model gun as quick as he asked.

He balanced it, played its hammer and trigger like he was tuning a fiddle.

'I can do what another can.' He tucked it in his broad belt. He had my spectacles and my gun now. I was being boned like a fish. 'I shall play your father and allot upon selling these things stalwart as I can be. Let us off the road.' He kicked his horse on.

I looked at spring about me, up to the sun. Behind us the ferry that cut our journey, and I saw in my mind four horsemen waiting for it to come across. They could not perceive that I would take the harder road. This was how I could beat him. Cheat him and set the law at him. And should he find me before I could do the right thing he did not know that I had Henry Stands in front of me. And a little of me hoped that that might happen, the same way on stormy nights you hope, just a little bit, that it might get worse before it gets better.

FIFTEEN

From southeast to northeast across Luzerne county are the Shawnee and Lackawannock ranges. They bisect the land, and about six miles parallel from these are the Wyoming and Moosic. These four mountains are like the pepper and salt pots that a man in a barroom will use to weigh down a map to plot his next day's ride. And in between these corner-set pots, as God looks down on the map, is the Wyoming valley that even people who have never seen it are familiar to sing about around a piano. It has a beauty in winter, spring, and summer that you do not have to look for, but it is crowded more than you think.

In ten years the mines had doubled the population, but as I said, when these patch-towns' owners ran out, the people found it hard. Harder still now the whole country was suffering and anthracite land is no good for farming.

Henry Stands's notion was to skirt the Nescopeck and Berks mountains and meet the Wilkes-Barre road, which we could ride to Stroud. And then, *God, I am nearly home!* This detour would count for nothing! Any way you tossed it I was little more than sixty miles to Stroud and then the Delaware and home. My aunt Mary's face was almost welcoming.

'This is a stage road,' Henry called back to me. 'Although they are not on my map, there are towns. There is one that begins with *S* that I cannot remember. Lot of towns begin with *S*. That is the Dutch for you. Even the president is Dutch now.'

He yawed like a ship as his stud picked a path upward and I watched both their rumps rolling in front of me. It was easygoing as the ground was good, which was for the best as Jude Brown was no Conestoga. Those were the big horses that pulled the canal barges and those huge Lancaster county wagons all across Pennsylvania to the sea, before the railroads. Funny how you never hear about obsolete things, obsolete people. Those horses and their drovers gone in a puff of steam. I guess there is not a lot of usury and subsidy in a man with a team of horses or a coal mine that serves only a couple of towns.

'I need rum,' Henry declared, but happy with it, as if the rum were coming just by saying so. I reckon he liked this country for its trees and birds and I did not blame him. It was beautiful and I do not use that word lightly anymore.

We came out into a mud plain and to a three-story

building that looked like a church and hid other houses and workplaces. A grist and corn mill stood on the side of a hill as they do them in the mining towns.

I would say that the menfolk of such towns spend so much of their days sloping down to work that they must like coming uphill all the way for their houses and stores. You have to be quite determined to settle if you do it on uneven ground with your house against a hill.

The church turned out to be the hotel and general store. It was strange to give it that pediment roof that gave it a holy air. Maybe it had started with grander ambition.

There were a few men in stained overalls and long hair milling around the mud street and I remembered that it had rained the night before, the night Henry Stands ran out on me.

He swung off his horse at the hotel post but I stayed, not liking the look of the whole place.

'Mister Stands, do we have to do this? Did you not get enough food at Mister Baker's for your journey?'

He staggered as the feel of the horse left him but it added to his surprised air at me.

'I was not expecting *you* when I made my stores! I was not expecting to stop for *every* dinner and *every* supper and to wet up *every* tree between Mifflin and Monroe! Get down. We need a stake.' He snapped down his gray coat and brushed it of its salt and road.

'How do I look?' he mumbled.

'You should remove your hat,' I said.

'Why would I do that?'

'It will make you seem humble and less like a forester.'

He took off his old headpiece and stuffed it under the

pommel of his saddle. 'How about now?' He gazed off to the left as if posing for a portrait, his right hand set across his belly. I reached up and he bent his head as I straightened and smoothed his hair. It was greasy but I expected that and it did not hang together but in strands of gray and black.

'I have a bow to tie it if that would help,' he volunteered.

He would not kneel, but he put me back up on Jude Brown and I tied his hair about his neck as neat as I could and he made as much fuss as if it were a terrier I was plaiting.

'Give me your book,' he said when I was done. 'Mind your horse.'

'You cannot go in alone.'

'And why is that?'

'You will need help. It is better as a two-man endeavor. My'—I did not say the word and Henry Stands did not need me to—'nearly always took me on the road. Door to door, as we say.' My eye was drawn by four horsemen on the mud road behind Henry Stands, and I guess I went pale. Henry rolled his head and followed my wide eyes but dismissed the old men the same as my sigh did a moment later.

'Well,' he breathed. 'I reckon I could use some assistance from an old hand.'

We set toward the store and I beset to babbling.

'You should buy something first, something small, and ask for some water for me. That will set his mind at rest.'

'You should have water and gin or small beer. You may find water alone to disaffect your stomach around here.'

I did not pay his words any mind and prattled on in my teachings. 'The guns are ten dollars wholesale. This is an opening offer, an exclusive; he will like that. He can sell them for whatever he pleases.'

'Ten dollars is mighty cheap.'

'That is wholesale. You do not understand these things.'

We mounted the porch. There was a disreputable fellow leaning on the post at the other end with a corn-pipe. I say disreputable because he had no hat or shirt, just his undershirt and braces over britches too short for his boots. He had a long knife in his belt but I took that as nothing: the boys and gangs in New York carried knives that could slit a horse's barrel.

He nodded at Henry Stands, who nodded back after surmising him also. We entered the store, which was cheap for windows, for it was dark as a barn with lamps that flickered with poor oil. There were four round tables set about, each with a single man drinking from jugs alone as if they were foreign knights who did not have the tongue to sit and talk together. They eyed us once and looked down to their cuffs or mugs.

Once in I became aware of Henry Stands's smell, which was profuse. I had bathed and had clean clothes. He stank of damp, fire, and road and not a little of rum. This is not how a salesman should present himself but I had small hope of doing business anyways. A cup of water was all I was expecting.

But Henry Stands had been holding out on me. I had forgotten who I rode with.

'*Irish!*' he called to the man behind the counter, which was not more than two dining tables boarded at the front with wood. I thought this opening an insult, but as it was the man grinned.

He wore a felted cap two sizes too big for him and a collarless shirt. A fat mustache made him seem friendly and furious in an instant but it was the friendly look that settled me.

'Henry Stands!' He stood up tall. 'Long time.'

'Not long enough, Irish.' We strode up to them nailed dining tables. I guessed that 'Irish' was not the man's real name, but the Irish were the first to come out here for the mines and the iron. He began to pour before Henry Stands had put his palms to the bar.

'Can I get some water for the boy? Clean as you can without paying for it.'

Irish gave me some gin in the water and I grimaced but he smiled and hacked with a tremendous blade at half a sugarloaf he had on the bar. He dropped a sliver in the glass and gave me a pine stick to stir it.

I thanked him but was unable to remove my down-turned mouth.

'What you doing around, Henry?'

Henry took his drink in one and pushed for more. I did not think this a good start for a salesman.

'I am to Cherry Hill for escapees. You don't know any escapees 'fore I get, do you, Irish?'

The man pretended to think for a moment. 'I do not.' He filled the shot glass again. 'What is with the boy?'

'I am returning him to my sister in Phillipsburg. He has been educated in Danville for a while.'

I did not reveal my astonishment at these lies. I felt safer for them. These were good lies. Henry was adept at them.

'But I am also on to Paterson, New Jersey, to fulfill orders on a new trade I have lucked into.'

'What trade is that, Henry?'

Not a bad hook fashioned. I supped my gin-water.

'Well, I suppose my chief will not mind me showing you, Irish.' He took out the wooden gun and displayed it wrist first. In the gloom it was impossible to distinguish wood from iron and Irish's face stiffened and Henry Stands snorted.

'It is just wood, Irish. A model for sales. Take a look at it.'

He took the model, gentle like a young girl's hand. 'So it is.'

Henry wiped his nose with his finger and then his brow with the same. 'It is a new gun. It is five shots in the fist. But reliable and machine made. A revolving gun but cranked by itself like clockwork. I have fired it many times myself and resolved to undertaking them for my own guns.'

I piped up over my glass. 'It is the future! Manufactured by Mister Samuel Colt in Paterson, New Jersey, sir!'

Irish looked at me, the gun in his hand. I smiled and he smiled back and winked as Irishmen do before they give you a small coin, but I did not get a coin.

'You use these, Henry?'

Henry plucked it back. 'Let me show you how.' He turned on the room.

'Gentlemen,' he addressed the lone drinkers. 'I have a wooden model gun here in my right hand. It does not shoot, it will not shoot. Take no offense, but I will use you in demonstration. You do not have to stand, but if you have pistol, rifle, or knife about you, draw it now. For show *only*. This is just a piece for Irish here.'

The four men looked from Henry Stands to each other. Henry showed the gun in an open palm. 'It is wood only! I wish you to throw down on me, without firing, if you will, and I will show you how this magnificent piece is . . . that is to say . . . how it is . . . magnificent. As I say.'

I watched the men still not stir and then I looked at Henry Stands and empathized with them. It was the holsters on his belt. I coughed and pointed to his waist.

Henry looked down and muttered through his beard as he emptied his belt and slapped his pistols to the counter and turned back on his audience.

'Now. Throw down on me.'

Slowly the men's hands went beneath the tables, their eyes moving from the real pistols on the counter to one another to a wooden toy in a fat fist.

A hand and a dark blade came up on the left.

And that was all Henry Stands needed.

He flashed the wooden gun at the hand and before I had time to blink he fanned his left palm over the hammer four times before anyone had cleared the table's surface.

The faint noise was only four flat cracks of wood against wood that almost sounded as one. The only cloud was the show of dust from Henry Stands's boots as he shifted to fire. The gentleman at the last table was so startled by the imaginary shot and fire that he dropped his pistol to the floor and apologized to Henry Stands for doing so.

I clenched my fist and punched the counter secretly to myself. The shots were quieter than his wind-rifle but no less impressive.

Henry Stands had demonstrated the Paterson as a shootist would, as the gun should only be shown, and some pity for that. It was a killing tool after all and a right fast and deadly one in the right, or wrong, hands. For street-work. I doubted that even mister Colt knew that his revolving cylinder could be utilized so.

Henry Stands thanked them sullenly and spun back to the counter and dropped the gun to its whiskey-sticky surface.

'There now, Irish. What you make of that? Four desperate men shot and saved from their wives in a heartbeat!'

'That is very impressive, Henry.'

'You can bet your mother it is. I have a letter from President Jackson affirming it.'

I jumped in. 'And barrels of them and revolving carbines have been sold to the Texas army! Our army and navy will take them up within the year!'

Henry nodded. 'And I am authorized to sell them for ten dollars apiece. Just two dollars' deposit—or trade—to confirm and you could sell them for three times that worth. You could have as many as you want in a month for they are factory made for quality and swift delivery. I have a book here full of orders. Take it or leave it. Take it or lose out to a man in Stoddartsville, where I will travel next.'

Henry Stands relished his new role. He had not looked at me to show any amusement but I had never heard him so verbose. He was as vocal as any of his birds. More so, as they only looked at each other silently across a page.

'How many would you like to take, Irish? I could do with some rum and potatoes and bacon for them.'

'I could do that, Henry. And I surely would.' Irish picked up the wooden piece and handed it back. 'I only regret that you were not here two days ago.'

Henry Stands's face became like stone; not a muscle moved as he spoke.

'Why is that?'

Irish grinned, or kept grinning, as I am not sure if he ever stopped from the time we entered. He reached below his bar-top and I saw Henry's fingers twitch to his pistols but they abated to see the reveal.

We could not have divined.

Irish raised and slammed to the wood beside the model its steel brother. Not a mark between them other than the nature of them, but there was no doubt that the steel one had a story ahead of ours to tell.

Henry Stands still stood solidified, but I stared at an explosion before me and drew away from the sight of the real gun that should not have been there.

Should not have been there!

I looked to the door. The dark of the saloon made it already the night. It was just afternoon. We could make hours before dark; we could run. Not yet in the night. Run. The daylight calling me.

Henry Stands's voice brought me back to stand as he spoke to Irish.

'Where did you get that?' he drawled but low and loaded enough that Irish would have to answer if he was to continue on.

'Two days gone. A young trader sold me two pistols of the same. He offered me Easton dollars in exchange for specie and if I gave three coins more for the guns.'

Henry Stands lolled his head at me and I read his mind.

Understand you that almost every county had its own paper notes. My father had taken notes issued from the Easton and Wilkes-Barre turnpike. You exchanged these for coin along the road and the canals. Easier to carry, the notes that is, but specie, actual coin, means more and always will. It is the metal of its worth. Do not let your government convince you otherwise or you are as lost as in a tornado with the paper whirling all around you. They will take it from you if you let them and charge you for its disappearance, hiding the coin behind their backs.

I stared at Henry Stands. These were my father's dollars, which only Thomas Heywood would have changed for coin or for food to feed his demon mouth. One of the guns lay silent on the counter. My father had been alive when I had known them last and the memory of that terror had the door pulling at my back and my legs moving. Only Henry's voice stayed me from running.

'Two days, you say?' He touched the barrel of the unique revolver. I noticed the men at the tables still paid attention, their eyes on Henry Stands's broad back, I guess not sure if their part had ended or not.

'Two days,' Irish said.

'You get the name of this man who sold them?' Henry asked quietly. His finger pushed the gun away for an inch.

'No,' Irish said. 'It was a good business. I did well enough to not ask names.'

I could not hold myself any longer.

'It was Thomas Heywood!' I yelled, and Henry glowered at me but I was riled with fear. 'Those are my father's guns! The man killed my father and took them and you have bought them from a murderer!'

'*Thomas!*' Henry bellowed with a raised hand set to side-winder me, but he was a length away. I was more thrown by his use of my name, his first yet. Still I backed away a step.

'Those are my father's guns!' My eyes blurred, and damn if my lip wasn't trembling, and I cursed myself and covered my jaw with my hand. 'You will give them back!'

Irish shook his head and studied me like I was in a cage. 'What is he about, Henry?'

'Never mind,' Henry growled, and stuffed the wooden Paterson in his belt and his pistols to their home. 'The boy is touched.'

He rushed on and grabbed my coat at my back and lifted me and I hung like a cat by its scruff as he strode to the door with laughter behind us.

I kicked the air and he shook me and I was out on the porch with the cold stinging my wet eyes and his rough face staring down at me. This was the closest I had been to that face. His beard was grayer up close and had bits like wool sprouting from his cheeks. The whites of his eyes were the same as the skin around them, like old, yellowed bruises.

'Who else sells those guns, boy?' He fixed me with a rheumy eye that bolted me to the wood under me. I could not lie. I had seen one other man in mister Colt's factory but that did not matter. I knew those guns. They were mine. I pulled my leather book with the linen pages from my coat and held it to his face.

'They are numbered, Mister Stands! In single figures! You see if the number of that gun does not match the first page of this book! You see if it don't!'

He straightened and plucked the book from me. 'Mind your tongue, boy.' He leafed through to the first pages and then looked over the edge of it down at my red eyes. 'I don't need to reckon on these numbers, do I?'

'No, sir.' I shook my head.

'Then we will suppose that your Thomas Heywood is on the road.' He looked about to the hills. 'Two days . . . Did your father have more Easton dollars?'

I did not know and I said so. I looked about also, every tree hiding a man in a saw-toothed coat or a hat with an Indian hatband. Henry must have seen my chest beating.

'Boy.' His tone was grim and he passed back the wooden gun from his belt. 'Don't be getting afraid on me now. I would not consider that kindly.'

I gathered myself and stuffed the model into my own belt. 'No, sir. But can we go?'

Henry Stands walked to the horses and I alongside. He was ruminating on our supplies. 'We have a murth of your sofkee. I will shoot a rabbit. We will do well enough with or without rum.' He paused and looked back to the store. 'Irish may take some powder for gin. I will try him.'

I thought of reminding him of the value of the

spectacles for trade but I was sure Henry Stands would not countenance such a sacrifice.

'You have anything else to trade, boy?'

I took out the brass compass.

'A bull's-eye watch?'

'A compass.'

Henry Stands kept walking. 'You are a curse.'

He straightened up the horses and checked his rifle's holster. 'Wait here. I'll take some powder and shot for Irish. I need only a handful for my pistols.'

'Where are we to go, Mister Stands?'

He made off to the store without an answer. He returned with two quart bottles, which he deposited in his coat, and as he mounted talked to me as if to himself.

'If your man has Easton dollars he will trade them along the road. He will go back to Wilkes Barre or on to Stoddartsville. I do not think he is out for you. Just coin and whiskey.'

'What about us?' I found a rock I could get up from and impressed myself with my single try to get on Jude Brown even with one hand on my wooden gun to stop it jumping.

Henry Stands wheeled his horse and looked up and down the road as if he could see for miles. 'Well, I think we will go higher. Go over the Lehigh river and through the shades.'

'The *shades*? The Shades of Death you spoke of?'

'I said I would. I said your man would not take the high ground.'

'None of that sounds promising.'

'None of this has been promising since I met you!'

133

He took out his wind-rifle in a single move that made me start and rested it across his stud's withers.

'You look out for a rabbit or something worth eating. You will need to look about fifty yards ahead all the time. He'll be gone else. Molly cottontails are not negotiable on the distance they will keep from you.'

We set off. East as always, the sun above us, but we took away from the road and went higher into the hills. I spent an hour looking down Jude Brown's neck instead of for a rabbit. I was reluctant to look up. I saw grass, then roots, then a blanket of pine needles go under Jude's hooves as the map changed around us. We had to duck for the most for the trees swiped at us. The light was lessened through the canopy all above. I was behind Henry Stands so he did not see me not looking for a rabbit.

I did not understand how I felt, but as I have become older, I have felt similar from time to time. Mostly late at night when sleep wants or in the dark moments before first light. A woeful sense of doubt that had nothing to do with my own ability or that of my sterling partner. *Inevitability* is not the word. It is drawn from the well of the indescribable. Like throwing dirt on a coffin or those moments when two men know that they are to fight each other and nothing more can be done except protect teeth and eyes.

I had no more crossroads. Standing across the ditch of the path I was digging was Thomas Heywood. He waited for me. And like all violent, laughing children (for that is still what his kind are even in their grown-up mind) they have nothing better to do than wait for you. In their reasoning there is nothing more diverting or entertaining than your misery. As children and as men they do not kiss good-bye to their families to go out for pleasant company or a drink and meal or for diversion. They go out to spread their misery. Good societies ostracize these felons eventually. But I was now aware that I was in the very lands that these men make their streets and homes when the good has had enough of them.

Henry Stands's wind-rifle cracked and broke my stupor. He had shot from the saddle, which is harder than you will suppose, and I looked up in time to see a rabbit fly up in the air like a fish hooked. The silence of Henry Stands's rifle was a godsend for hunting. It is hard to imagine now but apart from hunting deer and buffalo the flintlock muskets were a terrible weapon. There was a spark and a flat crack, a whoosh of powder and flame before anything left the barrel. Hangfire. *Trapping* was the word, and that was exactly it. You trapped game; you did not shoot it. Then there came that Scottish clergyman who grew so frustrated at birds escaping his flintlock fowling piece that he set to inventing, and the percussion cap and its fulminate powder made for a near-instant shot, but nothing could match Henry Stands's weapon of choice. He could shoot a duck and while its partners were wondering why their friend had just keeled over he could take them all like shucking corn.

'That was *your* task.' Henry discredited me from his horse. 'I am to do all the looking and shooting and the cleaning and the cooking, am I? Supposing I do all the eating?' He scowled at me and I took that to suggest that I was to fetch the rabbit.

The kill was uncommonly clean. Magical to come from a human device. A perfect round hole on the neck as the canine from a beast might do. Straight through.

The rabbit was in my arms, his mouth drawn, his eyes wide and still focused on the last thing he saw, his teeth dark and like tiny chips of stone. Everything about him dry. I could not help but compare the end of my father. A death sudden and fiery. A wet death. I trudged back.

'You seem displeased for him.' Henry put the rifle away.

'It was a good shot, sir.' That was my best. I held up the rabbit to him.

'No powder. No shot,' he said. 'You could eat him now if you wanted.' He took it and put it in his lap where his rifle had lain and stroked it like a cat as he rode on. 'He was beautiful. And will be so again in an hour or so.'

Henry paid no mind to whether I could get back up on Jude Brown as he went off but I was getting mighty good at spotting where I could dismount and get on by the ground and rocks. Jude had also begun to notice these things and sidled to them. Horses will marvel you just when you think them stupid as cattle.

We camped on a slope that had a creek at the bottom and lots of good flat rocks. We were in the trees and the grass and were well secluded, which I liked. It was still hours until dark but Henry Stands was of the mind that in the hills if you found a set you should make it rather than be stuck in the dark with no place to go later on.

Henry found a good stump-like boulder and the rabbit

136

slapped on the table, his white belly showing, and this bit I was dreading, but Henry saw my ill-face and gave his wicked smile, which he used when he felt that a lesson was in order.

He pulled out from one of the pouches about his belt a short double-edge, as thin as a sheet of paper and bright as a mirror.

'This is your skinning knife.' He twisted it before my eyes. 'You don't use it for anything else or you'll be buying another one.'

'Aren't you going to wash him first?'

He grunted. 'Ain't nothing cleaner than a rabbit.' He showed me the rear end. 'Clean as you when you were born. He has to be so to keep others from finding him.' Before I could look elsewhere he had nicked it around this area and between its legs where I guessed its business was.

'Now you go straight up like cutting cloth with scissors,' and he went up its white fur straight to its neck with a sound just like cutting cloth, as he said, and my mouth made an O with the simplicity of it.

'Then you peel him free.'

The fur came away like taking off a coat, no blood, and I was amazed, even smiled, and this pleased Henry.

'See. He don't mind. He knows he's for use.'

He cut it to its feet and minded me with a point of his knife. 'Now, you don't cut off his feet. You twist them off. You'll blunt any knife if you cut it and that will make an expensive meal.'

He twisted the bones and I did not like this and turned my head from the awful sound. I raised a question to cover his work.

137

'Have you never married, Mister Stands? You have no children?'

'You asked me before.'

'You said you were past liking women.'

He was cutting around the neck. 'Again, do not cut through the bone.' The rabbit was now a good deal thinner. Its inner side was a creamy white and it wore its fur like a cape as Henry went to work on its head.

'There was a woman,' he said as he admired the rabbit. 'And a boy.'

'A *boy*?' I was pleased.

'He died at six weeks old. I had newspapers that I had not thrown out that were older.'

'What happened?' I regretted asking this but the question came natural. He did not seem to mind.

'Oh, I had some money when I had done being a ranger. I told you I took my father's inheritance before he died to stay away from him. I played rough for months and met a girl who worked in a bank.'

'What was her name?'

'Mary.'

'That is my aunt's name!'

'It was not the same woman. I was a drinker and she was a drinker. We had a baby and rented a room above a newspaper office in Bend.'

'What happened?' I said again, and bit my lip at my repetition.

'Well.' Henry concentrated on the rabbit. 'He didn't eat. He didn't take the breast. He was sick every day. He was called Henry.'

'That is terrible.'

'No. It was. But these things go if you work on them.

138

It seemed foolish to have to bury such a small thing and people who didn't know him being sorry for you.'

'What about your wife?'

He wrenched the skull from the neck and gave me the head. It was bloody. 'Bury that a little or we will have disturbance in the night. We were not married. She left two days after. I wrote to her family when I sobered but never got no reply. As I said, I am done with women. Scratch a hole and put some leaves on that head. I will gut the body while you're gone so you do not raise your stomach hereabouts.'

I took the head in cupped hands and he dropped the four feet on top. I said, as politely as I could, 'I suppose six weeks is not a long time to get to know someone. That would have been easier.'

He wiped his hands on his coat, then seemed to regret it with a cuss. 'No. I knew him. You'd be surprised what you gather in such a time. Now be quick, we will need water next. I will use his guts for fuel. Don't look if it displeases you.'

I went uphill and knelt to scrape a hole. I put that head with the wide eyes and feet in the hole and covered it with the earth and some leaves and a stone on top to keep it so and paused to study it. It was a good grave for a small thing.

SIXTEEN

When I came back Henry Stands had chopped up the rest of the rabbit. I figured he would roast it but I guess he did not go for that or did not have the tools for it for he just dropped the pieces in the boiler and mixed it up with the sofkee and plenty of water for a stew of sorts.

He had made a good fire pit and the guts burned well and helped sharpen my hunger. It was still daylight and a daylight fire is very pretty. It is less welcoming than one in the dark but has the advantage that you are not blinded to see what is going on around, but it smoked a lot.

I looked up and watched the smoke going through the trees like a stack. I thought on the night with my father when I had looked up the mountain at those forester fires and felt companionship with them. I hoped there were not men now that looked up into the hills for fires.

Henry let the stew boil for a long time and took to his gin. He laid off his belt with his guns and leaned on his bedroll on an elbow and did not talk to me as he drank. We had not melted a block of tea so I just drank water from a canteen. I did not mind. I felt sorry for our talk earlier but I had nothing to say to make up for it. I just listened to the boiler bubble and hoped that that rabbit's family was not relying on him for anything.

I distracted myself with my future again. 'How are we to Stroud, Mister Stands?'

He stretched and sighed and swigged his bottle. 'We are just north of White Haven. Mining country. I think if we head southeast out of these hills and cross the Lehigh we will be into Monroe county and the shades. Tomorrow afternoon we will make it.'

I grinned. Stroud and the law and then the Delaware. Then New Jersey. Then home. To mister Colt first (I had no doubt about that no matter how much I missed my own bed), but two days and I would be in my home with my aunt and recount the terrors I had known. Comfort her in her tears for her brother-in-law, pat her shoulder as she rocked against me in her chair and I would say, 'There, there.'

She would worry about what we were to do. I would calm her worries. I could sell spectacles like my father. I could sell them by post. I could sell guns similarly for mister Colt now that I had the names of clients who would doubtlessly require return business.

We ate in twilight blue; there would be less flying insects to bother us that way, the fire yet to draw them. The birds were giving their final calls for the night and we left the horses free to eat of the grass. They grazed in a close circle like they were tying ribbons around us.

The rabbit was good and sweet like a cakebread but I would have liked to have made tea before we had used the boiler. Henry Stands must have sensed my need for something and passed over his gin. I dislike gin, as I have said, but in the open you will take anything to warm you and everything tastes better in the open air.

I gulped it—to try and not taste—and Henry Stands smiled at my grimacing blush as I passed it back. But the gin worked well in welcoming me to the night, and with the meal under it I felt warm and good.

The night came in and I still had some pieces of coal and put these in the wood-fire with some more kindling. I did this without bidding and Henry Stands watched me with a studious eye as if he had just seen me for the first time.

I sat on the blanket that I had taken from Jude Brown and took off my coat to use as a cushion of sorts. I stuck the wooden gun into the back of my belt for it stuck against my ribs when I sat. I hoped Henry Stands would have sympathy again and share some of his blankets with me.

This was only our second time sleeping out although it had something right familiar about it. I thought we had done it many times. I had become used to the sense of lying on the ground and of crackling fires and being in the company of only one other. I realized that this time had been more spent with my father and that was the real of it. I had lost all sense of time and days. Even now I could not tell you how long I had been gone from walls. My recall is mixed together like stirring paint. Two weeks almost or thereabouts, all encompassed in a day's worth of memories, which I am writing as if you asked me for a story after supper as we smoke cigars and drink labeled whiskey.

Henry corked his bottle and, still lying against his bedroll, began to sing. His voice was more like talking than singing, as if he was being forced to do so, and I had begun to think that this was one of the consequences of his drinking.

> 'Now soon some still Sunday morning
> The first thing the neighbors will know
> Their ears will be met with the warning
> To bury old Rosin the Bow
> My friends will so neatly dress me
> In linen as white as the snow
> And in my new coffin they'll press me
> And whisper, "Poor Rosin the Bow."'

He waved his bottle at me. 'Go tie the horses,' he said, and repeated his song, and I heard the cork pop again as I put my back to the fire.

My shadow came down the trees as I went to the horses, who were chewing and eyeing me. I had to move only ten feet away to lose the light and I took up their reins in a vagueness, each of them either side of me, Henry Stands's big stud making the night blacker. If anyone looked at us I would not be seen.

I looked out to the fire from under Jude Brown's head

and watched Henry Stands's neck go back with his bottle to the sky. That would be the end of one of them gins. I went to the saddle of his horse for the rope but never made it. *A hand on mine!*

A skinny arm hoisted me up and round and into the filthy face of Thomas Heywood, grinning at me like a skull.

I tried to yell but my throat had shrunk to nothing and he pulled me close so I could smell the whiskey on his breath and the sickly sourness of his clothes.

'Well, well, I've been following you like the moon, boy! I've been watching you sleeping,' he hissed. 'I found your wagon. Followed your horse.' He pushed me into the giggling belly of Indian-hatband, who dragged me away toward the trees.

God bless the horse of Henry Stands! Jude Brown just stood like a steer but Henry's horse leaped backward with his head whipping when the trash went for the wind-rifle's holster. Heywood cursed and let him go, then grabbed me again so I was held between the two by my shirt and hanging like meat.

Over the fire I watched Henry Stands rise at the commotion, but he stopped moving as the two other roadmen stepped to the fire with their rifles at their waists. His horse snorted to his side too late to warn him and resumed gnawing at the grass instead now his excitement was over. I will give Thomas Heywood and his boys some credit: they moved quietly when they had need to. Cowards do.

Henry Stands looked to his belt on the ground, and the two on him cocked guns to cool his thoughts.

With the fire amid I could see them only as half

144

figures, their faces under their hats just shadows, but I could see the silver hair and whiskers of one and the black coat and lifted collar of the other, he who I had perceived before as just coat and hat.

At the snapping of the rifles Heywood and Hatband threw down also, but their guns to my head.

I stared into the barrel of first one and then the other of my father's guns. Heywood pushed me forward, his fist tight on my collar, his knuckles against my neck.

'Don't move, old-timer!' Heywood put the cold steel hole on my cheek. 'Move and I kill the boy!'

Henry Stands scratched his beard, looked at all four of them, from boots to guns.

'Reckon you kill the boy whether I move or not.'

Heywood shook me. 'That's a fact. But how it happens is up to you. Shoot him in the face. Quick for him. Or hang him in front of you. Slow for you both. Which will you have?'

Henry lowered his face, now black under his hat-brim. 'You lousy son of a bitch.'

And Henry reached down for his belt.

'I said stop, you bastard!' Thomas Heywood fired high into the trees, shot to warn, to tremor the wood and our nerve. The birds woke again. Jude Brown reared away and to Henry's stud for protection, and Henry stopped moving as the rifles went to shoulders.

Henry Stands straightened, sucked in his gut, and raised his chin.

'So you be Thomas Heywood? The bravado that shot the boy's father in the back? Or are you some other nameless son of a bitch?'

Heywood brought the gun back down to my head.

'Well, ain't that digging your own grave, old-timer. That's a bad step. Bad step. I was just going to take the boy. You scratched yourself now. You know my name. That's not good. Not good at all. You leave me no choice, mister. No choice. I would have to save my neck.'

'We've already gone to the law, son. Judge Tanner in Danville. Marshals are out for you. You thought on that? You put up now and you might get good jail-time. Any more killing won't go better.' He turned to the others. 'And you boys. No-one's looking for you. No sense in letting this sorry bastard hang you. Clear out.'

He spoke as if that were the only thing for them to do, as if he had known them all his life, their trusted friend. The rifles pointed at him were just candy canes that he had given them as appeasements. 'Think about that,' he advised.

I could not see if they contemplated and it was Heywood who spoke for them.

'Go through his bags. See if he's got any papers from the law,' he said. 'Get his rifle and powder. If he moves, shoot him so he can't walk.' He put his gun to Henry. 'And I'll shoot the boy in the belly with his own guns. And you can watch him die. Might take days if I do it right.'

I wanted to say dozens of things but I was numb. I moved my frozen face from Henry to Heywood, to the fire, to my feet, and the play went around without me.

Henry did not move and I watched Silver-hair go to the stud. Henry never looked at me, I was sure. He watched everything but me, his head steady on Heywood, as Silver-hair went through his saddlebags one-handed, his gun still trained with the other.

146

Silver-hair pulled out Henry's leather book, let it fall. It opened out on the ground to show us the discordant pleasing forms within and Silver-hair cocked his head to it.

'*Birds!*' He laughed. 'Hey, Tom! Look at that!' he said. 'The old man likes to draw birds!' His hand went further through the bag and took out the string-bound pencils. 'He has pretty pencils too!'

Heywood haw-hawed. 'Is that ribbons tying them up?'

Black-coat did not laugh. In his black form he kept his piece solid on Henry, and Henry kept himself straight and patient because of it. I think they measured each other well. In any group there is always one who knows his business.

But I could hold out no longer. I could do nothing to defend my situation but I found my voice to Thomas Heywood.

'That is my book! My drawings! Little you know about anything, you son of a bitch!'

Hatband giggled faster and Heywood striped me with the pistol across my head, and my legs went light.

'You little bastard!' he spat, and raised to hit me harder.

'Hold there,' Henry said calmly, and Heywood quit his blow.

Henry Stands took a step.

'We all know you can shoot men in the back and want to kill their children. How are you against a real bastard?'

He moved farther, ignoring the iron on him. They let him come.

'I know I don't have a problem'—Heywood leveled the Colt—'killing an old man.'

The gun did nothing to stall.

'Yes, I'm old,' Henry said, and folded his arms. 'Old enough to have made cemeteries of men younger than you. Killed in wars. Killed in peace. Knifed and shot my way most of my life. Killed Indians and white men with my hands or the guns I took from them.'

Another step, his arms unfolded.

'I get paid to bring in escaped men that have done worse.'

One more foot.

'And there is nothing in you that don't stand thin against me, and you know it. And this ain't the first time I've had guns against me and you know that too.'

He looked at them all, weighed them all.

'And I'm done talking.'

He came past the fire, stolidly forward at two pistol mouths and two rifles, and I guess they did not know what to do for they stayed their hands. The two riflemen looked to Heywood, and he answered with cocking the despicable, treacherous Colt again, and though this made no difference to him in his coming on, I would not see Henry Stands cut down. I would not. I would not see such again. I could not help him either. But I would not see it.

I kicked at Heywood's shin, as children do. He howled and I broke free. He fired uselessly to the ground. I wrenched myself from Hatband and streaked into the woods.

I ran.

I heard shots behind. A booming discharge ringing

off the rocks, or the conflagration of Hell striving to claw me back to what I deserved. My rhadamanthine judgment.

Still, I ran.

'And now, ladies and gentlemen.' The ringmaster in the tall silk hat circles, his white greasepaint glowing.

'I show you the worst of Thomas Walker's crimes. His worst testament against. His judgment not for us but for a higher order.'

He pulls back the curtain and a white lantern shines on a whiter body standing naked and alone and bloodied like the Lord, but dying of more than his wounds.

'I give you his abandonment of Henry Stands for your scrutiny and horror. His savior and guardian. Left to the wolves. Left while Thomas Walker flees for his life.' He holds out his hat.

'It is only one more cent to see more.'

I ran and scrambled upward. I could hear voices. My shirt and knees were wet with the ground as I slithered to mount rocks and mud where their horses could not go.

The wooden thing slipped from my belt and tumbled below. I reached after it but it mocked me with its skill to tumble over itself. I could just make it out against the leaves.

I could hear nothing, could see nothing except my own body in the pitch, but I knew I was only a shout and one good look away from it all. Leave it. I should leave it. It had been nothing but trouble.

I slid back down and found it with my foot. I could

hear them coming; the trees shook with them. I reached down and brushed the gun clean and tucked it behind me again. Higher was hope. Think of where fat men will slip and curse and convince themselves that boys will get lost and starve alone and forget about them.

I was on a trail, a path. A wall of rock all along, pale now as the moon came over the hills as I went higher. The stone giant and square with flat tables above. If I could climb up there it could take them hours to follow. They would have to work round with the horses or if on foot, and huffing and slipping, they could not go where boys could. The advantage to the child. Endless energy when fear comes and the whole world just a place to hide.

The Lord helped me up. I climbed rock formed when he made the earth and yet it seemed each crevice and pattern in it had been designed with careful thought for this night and my escape and the moon just peaking the trees and lighting just enough to show me each step to take.

I reached the plateau but still climbed forward on my belly for a few yards so I would not be near the edge when I stood to be framed against the sky for a lucky shot. I got up and looked about. The ground before was made up of white broken rock like the metaled road of a titan.

I stepped, and the stones complained and moved under my foot, but I went on. Once or twice I heard a rattle and changed my footing but kept heading forward for the higher ground and the trees.

I did not think about earlier. I spoke to myself, talked to my feet and rubbed my arms. I had left my coat and hat,

150

and the wind was flintlike as I went higher, but it would be better in the cover of the trees. Everything would be better in the cover of the trees. I thought only on the importance of the moment, realized that was the way I had got through all things until now. What was important was that my belly was full, I was not tired, and I was alive. That much was right. An hour or so later and I had improved on that even: I was alone. And although I knew that was bad, the trees were my church and sanctuary.

I had evaded.

SEVENTEEN

I had my compass and I talked to it when I did not talk to my feet. I put it close to my face and angled it to the moon's light. I asked it where I was and it showed me north and so gestured me east and I was not that green to know that if I went down and hit a creek I would hit a river and a town soon enough or at least a grist mill with some kindly gentleman.

I did contemplate and asked the compass if there was not too much iron in these hills to differ but he reminded me that the moon was going east to west and I could judge him by that.

But I would need shelter soon and the night agreed with me on that as I felt rain on my cheek and looked up to see nothing above, but over my shoulder clouds were chasing the moon and me.

I went on, stopped and caught my breath when I needed, for I was still heading upward, which was wearing me down, but the rain caught up on me and despite the trees I was cold and wet by the next time I broke cover. The moon got blanketed and put me in a hole of blackness.

I stumbled along with one hand feeling along rock, against trunk, and inched my feet like I was stepping on ice, but this was good for I was confident I could not be followed.

I had put more than a good couple of hours behind me but my woolen clothes got real soaked and I began to shiver against my bones. That would not go well if I did not find somewhere to hide.

I recalled Henry Stands had described this land as anthracite rich and I had passed a few slits like evil mouths in the rock, not big enough for me to rest in but ably suited for snakes. I hoped for a path that might lead to a mine, abandoned for my best hopes as Henry Stands had said they often were.

As I thought and hoped on this I slipped and landed my rump hard on a rock. It was a foolish injury that would have brought loud laughter from anyone watching but it hurt like hell and soured me further. Pains on my head from the lumping Thomas Heywood gave me, and now an aching rear and muddied clothes.

Maybe this was some holy intervention to keep my mind off deeper troubles. Sometimes I guess the Lord can only do little things to ease, and pain is one of those. I rubbed the back of me but the wet and cold gave no comfort and I concentrated on it so much that it was some time before I noticed I was on a dirt path, overgrown for sure, but civilization had been here and my tripping over a wooden track made my heart leap.

I followed the cart-track and was surprised and welcomed by the rubbing and mewing of a cat at my legs. I walked on and was joined by another, who led me down the track flicking its tail at me. Neither of them seemed bothered by the rain and this encouraged me.

At the turning of a bush that had grown at head height over the track I came to a sanguineous glowing blanket suspended in midair across the path. Closer and I saw it was a brattice covering across the opening of a mine and a lamp within shining through.

I hurried forward and then stopped with the cats spiraling around my feet. The lamp meant someone was behind that curtain. My immediate past meant that I distrusted even the natural world, let alone the hands of men in it.

But Henry Stands had been a good bad man. There could be others. I am sure I had known more good men than bad and you have too so that is how you should measure the world if it came down to numbers, as it might, come Judgment.

I approached the curtain.

'Hullo?' I called, and the cats echoed me with their little voices.

A long drag of silence, then the rattle of pots and a crooked silhouette rose on the curtain and I saw arms bend to a head in a fright.

'Who's it there?' a voice croaked. An old voice, and I relaxed but not knowing why. 'Who's it there? Them's my cats.'

'My name is Thomas Walker. I am no harm.'

The shape on the curtain grew larger. 'What you want?'

'Shelter. I should like to wait until dawn. I ask nothing else. I am a boy.'

The curtain whipped across and a bald head and face met mine. 'Lost? Lost, you say?'

I had not used this word.

He was old. And thin. Big eyes like a catfish, too big for his head, which was concave at every bone and swayed on his neck as if too heavy to bear. He wore no shirt but a leather waistcoat that showed his skeletal chest and arms. I was satisfied that he was not stronger than me and very old to boot. His suspicion lightened when he saw I was a boy, and he smiled kindly and I could see the younger man within him then.

'Son.' He pitied. 'You are drowned. Come in. My cats have found you. They must think you have bacon about!'

He took my arm and drew me under the curtain. I thanked him but looked around before proper introduction. His lodging was but nine feet wide, the width of a mine-car and track, and tall as a big man. This was the entrance, the adit, of a strip mine. A strip mine cuts from the mountain rather than being a shaft down into the earth. This old man lived in the slope that might have been the office in its past for it had cupboards and furniture. Another brattice down the slope testified to the mine proper. He had made a good job of it. There were shelves both cut out of the rock and hung, and a canvas cot and a proper stone oven with a rusty tin stack disappearing into a wall. He had food boiling that smelled salty and good and the blue smoke smarted but was welcoming. It reminded of civilization.

He had oddments and mess everywhere and I could not take much in before he began to straighten his home and be as hospitable as a man in a cave could be.

I have found that the more humble a man's circumstance the more he will put himself out and offer comfort. I have sat in great halls and been offered not even a sip of water despite being invited to attend, and I have visited one-room shacks unannounced and been welcome to the first slice of everything and the last finger of whiskey and even a man's bed. You know I am right about that because it has happened to you too. For the rich folks it usually starts with the words 'Help yourself,' but those words are the precursors to 'but' and 'should not' and 'we do not usually' and you get sent out into the wet night hungry and dry throated. There is a reason why they are rich.

'Who you say you were?' he asked, and I could look at him better now in the isinglass lantern light. He was not much bigger than me but he did stoop so it was hard to tell. He had proper trousers and braces and good boots and never stopped moving, tidying up the place of what seemed like trinkets and charms, stones and Indian-like things, even when he was listening to me.

'Thomas Walker, sir. Thank you for letting me in.'

He scoffed at my thanks humbly like I was giving him a gift on Christmas Eve and offered me a seat, which was a half barrel upturned.

'But you are soaked, boy!' he declared. 'Why you out on your own? Best get some dry clothes. I have plenty. Why out here on your ownsome?'

'I am not alone,' I lied. This was my defense. I have

156

said before that I distrust anyone who does not have a key to my house and I see no reason no to do so until you see how another fellow travels and courts. It was the same for me with Henry Stands and so it would be with this old boy.

'I went for a walk when it was dry and have become separated from my party. In the morning I shall be fine. I can find my own way.'

The two cats had become four, of different colors and, in the light, of different stages of missing fur and half-closed eyes or chewed ears. They rubbed against the old man and he stroked and kissed his lips at them as he spoke.

'Well, you are welcome, Thomas Walker. I will get you clothes and dry yours on my coal. I am Strother Gore. Pleased to meet. I am want of company.'

I nodded, my shivering getting worse with the warmth of the cave, and I could not speak much further for the chattering of my teeth.

'A blanket,' he said. 'Yes, a blanket.' He scurried away and brought one to me. 'Get undressed beneath, for your shame.' He laughed and I noted his gapped teeth, which made his chortle like that of an infant and drowned the sound of rain outside the curtain. I thought of speaking of my troubles, a Christian warning. This old man did not deserve the retribution due to me. But my own preservation this night was a hill above my charity. Outside, behind that curtain and through the rain, I was sure I was sought, and if he was made aware Strother Gore might decide that he did not need the troubles of a small boy.

'And clothes,' he said. 'I got lots of clothes.' He laughed

157

away again and carried back from a hidden corner britches and a blue capote shirt. They smelled musty and aged but fitted good, though why he would have such to fit me I did not ask.

Mister Gore paid me no mind as I changed. He tended to his late supper and shushed the cats away with giggles and admonishments until each knew how good or bad he was and closed their eyes and grinned or ducked and dashed accordingly.

I thought it late to be eating but I did not know how late. I had eaten hours ago and thought we were now in early morning, but Strother was not eating; he was stirring only and paying even that little mind. I put the Paterson on the barrel and he stared but he saw that its pattern matched the wooden seat.

'That is quite a toy,' he said. 'Did your father make it?'

I looked at the gun. 'Yes. No. He gave it to me.'

'What is that round bit of it?'

'It is a revolving cylinder of chambers,' I quoted. 'For five shots.'

'I have never seen a gun like that.' But he ended the conversation on that statement.

He took my clothes and hung them over a cord above his oven, talking to each of my garments in turn with tuts and whistles. I was still wet across my shoulders but the blanket, his stove, and the closeness of the cave had dried the rest of me. I was good again.

'You hungry?' He leaned over to me with one eye squinting.

'No, sir.'

'I have a stew?'

'I have had supper. Thank you. With my family.'

'How about some johnnycakes? Honey in them now there are bees again. And tea?'

'That would be welcome, sir. I can bring you some tea tomorrow and some other goods for your kindness when I am back to my party.' This was a lie, naturally, but what harm?

He smiled with what teeth he had and with a pot already boiling poured me a tea. I thought we had come along enough to ask questions, especially as I was drinking and eating into his stores. He told me as he passed me the johnnycake that he baked them on a shovel, which was why they were so big, and he was not misleading, for it filled my entire hand.

'Do not worry,' he said. 'They are good. I am no clay-eater.'

I chewed and talked. His biscuit was good. 'You live here, Mister Gore?'

'Why wouldn't I?' he said, wide eyed and angry, and then smiled as apology for his snap. 'This is as good a place as any,' he said. He waved his spoon to his walls. 'I am happy here. There is no charge and I have lost my interest in towns. This place was a strip mine, as was. It ran out more than ten years gone. I did work it in its prime. It holds enough fuel for my little uses. Not enough worth for anyone to dig further. I think the town has all gone by now.'

'Have you been here long?' He did not seem to like this question so I changed my line. 'It is impressive what you have done with it, I mean. It is most comfortable. And, as you say, free of charge.'

He pointed his spoon at me. 'You know what *mortgage* means? It is French. It means "dead pledge." It means you are in debt and are not expected to pay it back except until after you die, when they will take your house and land and sell it again.' He went back to his stirring. 'You know how many people I have seen, families I have seen, run off their land by landlords. *Landlords!* Bah! *Banks,* you say? Bah! Landlords are but patient bailiffs. And do you know what bailiffs are? In the old countries they was the despised, the pardoned criminal, the foreigner. No decent man. But here? Here they have fine suits and hats, offices and brick houses. What befalls this country when we give respect and due to people who would take your arm and sell it back to you!'

This was angry talk, and fast, with spittle at his mouth, and the staring he gave me as he ranted unnerved me. He had said that he had worked this mine and I supposed there was an event in his past that had embittered him.

I knew nothing of mortgages and landlords and until I met Strother Gore I thought that everyone had a home. Those folks I had seen camped outside Milton were there from choice, I had thought. I would not chase to upset mister Gore further; he had become ugly and muttered into his stew and even his cats moved away. I ate on my biscuit and sipped my tea. My developing knack of upsetting folks was inclining me to return to my ways of sitting quietly and leaving adults to the world. A flash of my father at the dining table with his newspaper came to me. My mother's shoes tapping on the tiled floor, my plate half-empty and me prattling on for water or talking about gas lamps or stars or anything.

My father flapped his newspaper down and glowered at me.

'Less talking and more eating,' he said, then shook it back up, satisfied that his point was made. My mother stroked my head as she put a glass of milk beside my hand and touched my father's hair also as she went back to the kitchen. It may have been raining then, which is why I had so thought of it. I kept to my father's order now and ate in silence.

'You are very lucky.' Strother Gore left his spoon to his pot and sat in front of me. 'Terrible things have happened in these hills.' He shook his head and looked to a corner as if remembering. 'Terrible things.'

'What things?' I asked, and saw him grin. I would indulge him his stories and he seemed to squeeze himself in anticipation. I reckoned the world had long stopped listening to him. Besides, I could use distracting now that the little things of pain and cold had died away and I had begun to think about what I had left behind or carried with me. Both are the same.

I touched my head where Heywood had struck me. I had not seen my face since that morning at Mrs Carteret's—Lord! That was only this very morning! My whole world had changed again before the moon had risen on the day.

I wondered if I was marked by the gun but Strother Gore had not mentioned. Then again, are not all boys bruised and cut most days, though they might have had more fun in the gaining of them?

'Terrible things', he said again, 'happen to children in these parts.' He looked to the curtain sucking in and out with the wind like a luffing sail. A brattice cloth is heavy, layers thick, they can hold back fire for a time; it would take a hurricane to bother it.

161

'*Indians!*' Strother Gore clapped his hands and giggled at my jump. 'Indians have been taking children in Pennsylvania for hundred years and more. You are lucky I found you.'

I did not correct him about finding me, and I had seen something of Indians myself although it was more dreamlike than real.

'But they are all away from here now,' I said.

'That's what them governments want you to think. "All is well. All is safe." Tell that to Frances Slocum and her brother and all of them. Hundreds of them.'

'Why would they take children?'

He leaned forward and lowered his voice. 'They will take them to make up for their dead. If a warrior falls, someone's son, they will take a child to replace. If a child dies and they chance upon a white family, they will take a child to replace.' He rocked back and forth on these words, affirming them as absolutes.

'All around these parts it happened. And no-one ever sees them again.'

'Ever?' I said.

He rolled his shoulders. 'There was a girl,' he said. 'Must be nigh on fourteen years since she turned up. She'd been missing more than sixty years. Mary she was.'

I almost said again that this was my aunt's name but the last time I had said that I had been with Henry Stands and I was trying not to think of it.

'Girl taken just last year there was. In Texas. Nine she be. *Was*. How old are you?'

'Twelve.'

'And small.' He looked me over. 'I reckon an Indian

162

could still pick you up and carry you away.' He said again, 'You lucky I found you.'

He began to rock more on his stool, hugging himself against the night air. I wondered why he did not dress more. He had given me a capote shirt. He must have had warmer clothes than the leather waistcoat he wore over his bones.

'Do you think this rain will stop, Mister Gore?' I said for want of anything else. I had heard adults talk of the weather to break silences between courses and coffee.

'It always has,' he said. 'Do you like your tea?'

I brought the cup to my lips. 'Very much so. Thank you, sir.'

He stopped rocking and waved to his bed against the stone wall. 'You may take my cot if you wants to sleep. I did not mean to frighten you about the Indians.' He hugged his knees. 'I am want of talking to folks.'

'I cannot take your bed, Mister Gore. I will prop this barrel to the wall and sleep with a blanket. I have slept on a wagon and on the ground for nights now.'

In truth I had no intention to stay the whole night. I would keep an ear open for the rain to stop. I knew the Lehigh was to the east. Towns and the Delaware scant miles away and I was chased, after all.

'Do not let me keep you from your supper. I will rest.'

He cocked his head to me and I saw his wide eyes grow in the lantern light. 'I will eat in the morning now,' he said, and then pointed at my biscuit. 'It is good, no?'

'It is too kind and too much.' I smiled. 'Thank you, sir.'

'Well, if them politic men will teach anything it is that we must learn to cook for ourselves. They will not provide, yet we must pay for their own tables. How did that happen?'

He sprang up and went to his stove, stirring and cursing above it. He gave me another sorrowful look.

'I did not mean to frighten about the Indians. You sleep now. I will watch us.'

I assured him that I was fine and bigger within than I looked and he nodded and stirred his stew harder.

I moved the half tun to the wall. To my right was the stiff blanket over the adit, keeping back the night. In front was mister Gore's shelves and chattels, his implements swaying from the scaffold he had made under the tall roof. He had knives and hatchets, spoons and pots hanging off lanyards drilled through their handles all swinging above my head. He was well provisioned for ten, let alone one.

Pulling the blanket around, I reached for the wooden gun and drew it to my chest and smelled its oil. I aimed my feet toward the curtain and drew my knees up. I was sure that I would be too uncomfortable and aware of those stalking me to sleep. I closed my eyes for the first time since the hostler's place. But I did sleep.

And I awoke in the dark to the ring of steel and iron.

EIGHTEEN

My eyes shot open over the blanket across my nose. Left and right I scanned the room from the blanket's shield. I could feel my pupils widening and the nerves of my eyes moving and waking my brain, my heart in my throat.

Just the wind! My brain laughed and mocked.

See? it said. *It rattles the old man's pots and knives. No-one is coming, boy!* But I raised and looked about regardless. I was becoming preternaturally aware, as men do when they are stalked.

The window of the stove showed just a ribbon of red, weak above the coals. The isinglass shutters of the lantern, sat on a barrel, showed pinpricks of life and sketched out the cave.

Mister Gore had gone to his cot and there were round lumps all around him that must have been his pets.

I heard the rain next. Still there. Still shrouding me from those that hunted. A long night. Good. Daylight, I am sure, would show me like a diamond. And then the night not so good, as my wakefulness brought on a full bladder.

I tried to settle down with it, wait for the dawn, but that never does work, and the further you are away from the head the less it does.

I sat up to think on it. I could go outside the curtain, in the rain. No. I stood and reached for the shuttered lantern.

I would go down the mine to the other curtain. I was sure mister Gore relieved himself as such on occasion.

I took the lantern from the barrel and crept down to the mine proper, not wanting to wake my benefactor. If I would go far enough beyond the curtain, I was sure the natural damp and cold would not mind my water.

Gore's cats' eyes followed the lantern; even those asleep cocked one green reflected glance. The curtain was heavy; these things were weighted and made to hold back fire, as I said, but I managed it as quietly as I could.

There was a great stifled air at me. The lamp was before my face and I dared open one of the shutters, which jumped at the draft and illuminated enormously. I would find a wall, put the lamp down, and be at my appointed business and back to sleep before I was dry against my leg.

Creeping down the slope, I held the lamp above and my right arm out to feel for the wall. I imagined the hundreds of men who had been here before me, and as if in instinct of them I swung the lamp to seek their torches set into the walls. And there they were. Cold. Just as empty and without work as the men that set them.

I could smell the wood and the coal-fire of thirty years all around. That smell is ingrained even now and even with all your gas and good anthracite you can recall the black in your nostrils and under the hair of your skin. It takes only one fire and back you come again. The caveman wearing fur. But I just needed to unhitch my britches.

I sidled to the right, put the lantern to the ground, and held my hand out to check I was not about to wet something important to mister Gore or hit a ledge that would spray back at me.

My hands touched on things that were cold. You get to know that touch as you grow older. I have stood in churches with it in front of me and touched its brow on that long day when I buried my sons.

These things jiggled and rattled as my hands roamed and I drew back. There is nothing as lucid as putting your hand among human bones. The revulsion cold-burns your fingertips and you feel guilty somehow.

My foot touched the lantern and I needed to pick it up to see, I had to pick it up. I had paid my red cent to enter the tent, to see the grotesque, as you have, as we drink our labeled whiskey together, as you asked me for a story.

The circus curtain pulls away but the lurid paintings on the tent outside should be enough for imagination. The deformed and the twisted smiling through their misery with serpent's eyes and filed teeth. Turn away with just the tent's exterior. Do not pay to go within.

I swayed the lantern and it echoed back along a row of skulls. It still echoes back whenever I forget to light a lamp at twilight and must do so in the dark.

Their black eyes, perfect and pleading, mouths grinning and placid and welcoming me to join. I lowered the light to see cloth and bones. Piled here and there, loose like that, no order. A leg bone jammed in a perplexed mouth, gagging on the ludicrous.

I think I stepped back, my eyes accustomed. I could not know how many bodies, bits of bodies, maybe a dozen skulls and then those that were not quite skulls. I do not ever try to remember them.

As I said, I think I stepped back, but however it happened I felt a body behind and I whisked round and the lantern lit upward into Strother Gore's grin. He had more teeth now and his eyes were black. He said nothing. He had a bludgeon raised and a claw set to grab my collar.

'*Mister Stands!*' I yelled, calling out for names I had forsaken, but it did some trick as Strother's neck twisted behind him and I swung that lantern at his body and from my hand and ran down into the mine.

It was black and with my boots running I could not hear if I was being followed, but I had practice of being chased now, so I was bolder than most, I figured.

I scratched to a stop. Running down would be running to a wall. Up and out the only way. Up. Up past Strother Gore seeking me out, his spider-thin arms outstretched and sweeping for me, his catfish eyes hunting through the dark.

I ducked and went for the left wall but I hit the track and went down, winded. A secret blessing, for now I crawled quieter and when at the wall I got down flat and listened.

Nothing came but the draft over my head. Silence. But that was a lie. I just could not hear him creep.

I got up and crawled, good and quiet, but then I heard footsteps shuffling toward and I went down on my chest again.

Strother Gore was coming and giggling and kissing the air at the same time, calling me like one of his pets. He never used words. I guess that when it came down to his madness it was better for him not to. He would be human then.

I held my hand to my mouth and lay still. The only thing in my head was the stew that Strother had been boiling, and that bludgeon. He had knives and hatchets and all. That would have been the end of me. Maybe he did not like the bleeding, maybe it ruined things. I wished I could not think on it, and then I could not as I heard him close to me.

He skidded on the rough ground but he knew this place and I heard him step over the track, invisible as it was.

He moved past and I heard him scoop up some gravel and throw it in an arc. I heard the stones scattering off the walls. I figured him for something like a bat and that this was just another show that he had been in before. None of this was new to him. He was listening for the stones hitting me, listening for cloth instead of stone. He kissed his lips some more, then a grunt as he bent for more gravel.

My need now was to move, to cut for the curtain and the outside. No doubt I was faster than Strother Gore and he would not count that I, with all my tribulations, was becoming used to fear.

I began to rise as he moved on, but a small body brushed against me, a wet nose touched my cheek, and a tail went under my nose. I went down again. *Damn his cats!* Another one now found me out and writhed against my face. I elbowed them aside and they did what cats do and voiced their vexation or called to their food bearer. *What they must eat with this man! Them thinking of me for their bellies!*

I heard Strother Gore turn with a hiss. A venomous sound that I will never forget and still hear when I am far from my porch and alone in my fields and a ruffed grouse flies away from my plow.

I scrambled up and ran hell for leather, as marauders say. There was no doubt nor danger that I could make the curtain before him, but I knew that I would have to pause to haul it aside. I heard a frustrated howl chasing me.

I made the black curtain and pulled at it but it resisted with the draft against it and tried to push me back for its master.

I went down and beat at it to bully through, then a slavering gasp on me, his hooks on my sides, giggling as he tickled for a grip, but I screamed and kicked back and went under that curtain like a greased shoat and he made a hoo-hoo sound.

Now I was in the cave, but his laugh behind and another brattice to fight through and then what? The night. The rain. The Devil behind me.

I sprang for the curtain and, God help me, did I not spare a sight to look on that damned wooden gun sitting on the barrel. But the lustful breath behind pushed me on and I grabbed for the curtain as he prized on my boot and I was done. Lost.

I squealed and skipped against his grip. Skipping to save my life.

And the curtain swept aside.

And Henry Stands's ghost stood before me!

The rain cut him and his long coat out from the night and ran off him, down the brim of his hat like the beaded veil on Chinese emperors in books. Those veils represent the stars. The stars where the emperor comes from.

Henry Stands looked at me and then at Strother Gore frozen at my heel. Henry was soaked through, his whiskers combed with the rain so his mouth took the pose of a mountain lion's. He did only one thing as he held the curtain over his head and that was a boot to Strother Gore's face, showing him how little he was, and that fiend flew back all the way to his oven with a squeal.

A hand came over me and hauled me out into the night. Henry Stands delayed only to look me over. He dropped me and held the curtain like holding back a cage door.

'Go wait on the track,' he said. 'I will be along.'

I brushed the rain from my face. 'How will I know it'll be you?'

I do not know why I said those words.

He pulled his hat down against the rain. 'It'll be me,' he said, and I went as I was told.

And Henry Stands went under the curtain.

171

NINETEEN

I dodged under the rain, finding the path from where I had come, and on turning upward, even slipped on the same slate that had got me before. Not wanting to move farther, I sat and hid in a bush. I was wearing dead men's clothes, my own left in the cave and, God forgive, if I did not hope that Henry Stands would return with them, that he would think of me regardless of his contentions, and then, assured that he would not return at all, I sat convinced that I was destined to die in the wild and no-one would know of me. I would not become a man, and yet I had made steps in the world that had killed many.

Footsteps came through the mud and I braced back into my bush like a startled possum. The coat appeared, the hat low across its face, the whole figure drowned and weary as if coming scooped out of a river.

Mister Stands!

I rolled forward and jumped up into his path. 'Mister Stands!' I cried.

He wiped his hands on his black coat and pushed my shoulder. The runoff from his hat fell into my eyes.

'You didn't eat that stew, boy?'

'No,' I said. 'I had a biscuit.'

He brushed past and put his hand behind and I reached out for it but it was not his hand he wished me to take. The wooden pistol filled my palm and I took it. I looked down at it, heavy in my hand. He stopped a pace away, his long back to me.

I looked back on the path, thought about my own clothes as the rain hit my neck. The rain was easing now as the moon was going down and the dawn was blue. But I was cold.

'Mister Stands?' I said. 'I would get my clothes.' He kept his back to me, took off his hat, and shook off its reservoir of rain.

'Don't,' he said, putting his hat back. 'You'll dry soon. You have your hat and coat at the camp.'

'The camp?' I had almost forgotten. 'But . . .'

'You moved through the brush like a lame steer,' he said. 'I would be disappointed, son, if you thought me dead by that trash.'

'They are dead?' My voice exalted.

'No,' he said. 'Wait and I will tell. We can make tea at least.' He pushed aside branches to break our passage.

'Follow me down.'

*

I was at Henry Stands's back and he did not talk. As soon as we came to water he took off his coat and hat and rolled and knelt to wash. I noticed he had no weapons on him, no belt of leather pouches for even skinning knives, and for a moment I felt pity for Strother Gore.

'Mister Stands?' I was the first to voice. 'I'm sorry I ran.'

He did not hear, perhaps for the creek, or at least he said nothing and shook on his coat and planted his hat and set to walking.

He waved me closer and I yelled at the sight of Jude Brown tethered loose to a bush. Damn if that horse did not dance a little on the stones at the sight of me, then he remembered his offish nature and went back to his chewing while I hugged his neck.

'He helped find you.' Henry Stands walked past us. 'He could smell your stains.'

'I'm glad you came, Mister Stands.'

'I figured you'd go up,' he said. 'The rest was just your clumsy feet.'

'Thank you, Mister Stands,' I called to the back of his neck.

He threw me a look from his shoulder. 'Don't. I will be in this for the monies now. Your promised fee from your man Colt. I will need a stake to get to Cherry Hill. I have nothing left.'

It was morning when we got back to our little copse of trees. The fire pit was still smoking, our boiler above it, our beds still on the ground. It was like I had only just stepped out from another room, my hat and coat on the ground as if I had vanished out of them by a witch's spell. The only sound was the patter of the rain on the leaves and the only real sight was the steam coming off Henry Stands's dead horse.

I looked at the beast's hide, which was black and blue and red, a large piece of him gone from his leg and flank.

I stepped into the circle almost in wonder. I had not expected to ever see anything again so the trees and the white sky were all as if first seen, the morning painting the world anew. But the dead scene was discomposing.

'What happened to your horse, Mister Stands?'

He stood beside it, his head angled in a study. 'Pack your things,' he said. 'I will take the rigging and load them to your horse.'

'But how did he . . .?'

Henry spun on me. 'You want to know?' He did not yell but his voice was curt. 'You want to know how he died?'

I set to the fire and the boiler to keep myself low from Henry Stands's scowl. Tea would make the air better. I looked about our sparse camp and Henry stood over me and told of his night.

'Good for you that you ran,' he said. 'I could not have helped you.'

'What happened?'

He walked around the fire pit in the footsteps crushed in the grass, and as he spoke I could see the tale written in the scarred ground and ending in his dead black stud.

'They fired on me when you broke but that did

not matter. I know good shots that could not shoot themselves in the head in the dark over a fire. Cowards never make good shots. That is how battles are won.'

He stooped to pick up a long rod of steel, and with a start I saw it was the barrel of his wind-rifle. He looked along the length of it.

'They ran after you, or ran as I came at them. Then I went for the horse, for my rifle. Them other two commenced to firing with their guns but just as wild.' He brought the barrel to me.

'They must have shot the gun on my saddle. Hit the reservoir of air. I only know there was an explosion that knocked me cold. And this is the scene I awoke in.' He nodded to the horse now being sniffed at by Jude Brown. 'That's what done for the horse.'

I remembered the fit of uproar I had heard behind as I sprinted. Not Hell clawing at me. It was the rupture of Henry Stands's magnificent rifle, the compressed air exploding through a wild shot.

'The gun was old. Past its prime. That was an iron tank.' He set the barrel down. 'You must reckon that even iron must get old.'

I still could not look at him straight. I reached for the tinder box with the striker and char cloth. The kindling was wet but with the cloth and coal I would work on starting. It would keep me busy.

'It would have been quite a display. Enough to kill the horse. They must have thought the devil of it, thought me killed and gone after the others. Took the time to take my belt and guns. We have the ax and food at least.'

176

'What are we to do, Mister Stands?' And as I said it I began to dread that perhaps there was no longer a 'we' to consider.

He squatted at the fire. 'You will have my wool hat and make this fire and tea. I will get some powder to help and I will cut some steak from the horse.'

'I meant about the road . . . about them.'

He tipped back his hat. 'Well, they have stolen from me. I will say they do not have long to live.'

I looked into the fire pit and struck a flame at last and then my tears came again. I pulled out the wooden gun from behind my back and threw it to the ashes for kindling.

My words spat at it.

'That is the only dry wood we have.' I wiped my eyes. 'It should burn! It has given only bad luck!'

Henry reached in and plucked it from the ashes. 'Hold now. You have gone through a lot with that toy. You might regret burning it yet.'

'I hate it!'

'Well, now, maybe *I* have been through a lot with that toy and do not want it burned.'

'Your wind-rifle is gone! You had that in the war! You said it was older than you and I have destroyed it and killed your horse to boot! I have lost you all your guns and knives!'

I shot up, hid my filling eyes and brushed blowflies from the air that were getting fond of the horse and testing us for life.

'You did not do that,' he said. 'And if not for the destruction of the gun I might have been dead now and not have come for you.'

177

'And what of that? That man was going to *eat* me!'

Henry was brushing the ashes from the gun. 'Whist! There are lots of men like that in wilder places. Every trail has talk of foresters and mountain men doing the same. I know of ghouls who get arrested and jailed for that madness and fifteen years later set about the same as soon as they can.' He was not rubbing the ashes off the pistol but now more into it.

'Well, now,' he said, and put his hand to the boiler for the cold tea. He rubbed the mush of tea from the boiler along the barrel and cylinder of the gun and then held it in his fist by its grip and squinted at it to the sun with a long arm.

'What do you think that looks like?'

The gun was dappled black now. I wiped my eyes and looked at it with the same squint as he.

'It looks like iron,' I said.

'I reckon if you were in a darkened room . . . that looks like a real thing to me. Real enough.'

'Mister Stands?'

He got up and sought his broken barrel.

'Take this.' He put it in my hand. 'Tuck it over your arm.'

I rested it in the crook of my body.

'Hold it like business.'

I swung it to him, two-handed, and he rubbed his whiskers.

'That'll do.'

I let the barrel hang by my side. 'Mister Stands? You cannot consider going up against them with a wooden gun and a piece of one?'

'Make the tea,' he said. 'And don't be asking me

doubts.' He looked upon the wooden art of Sam Colt with new eyes.

'You should know by now, son, that the world began when I was born.'

TWENTY

Henry Stands walked us out of there, leading me on Jude Brown's back. We were still on a walking trail but Henry told me that we were between Stoddartsville and White Haven and he was keeping a count on the creeks we crossed and that before nightfall we would reach the Lehigh.

'You must've come something of this way?' he roared back at me. 'One would remember crossing the Lehigh. It is a place to see.'

'I . . . we came in at Stroud. We must have crossed it at a dull set. We went through Conyngham? Then to Berwick. It was five days. There was no wet country like this.' And that was true. Even the ground seemed alive although Henry informed me that this was but the edge of the Shades of Death. There were dead pools and dead trees but these were being pushed back by the young live ones of spring. But I was glad that it was open enough. You could see a man coming yesterday, as mister Stands would say.

'Your father must've went straight along the latitude. Guessing he had to with that wagon of yours.'

It did me no good to be reminded of my mother's wagon. Surely boys should have better peace than this? I thought I would never sleep again or know a day when my heart was not fluttering. And now Henry Stands would get us killed for his pride. I was too young to know about pride, only of its sinful attribute. I did not attach it to honor and I reckon that God made pride a sin to stop men like Henry Stands coming through his gates and showing him his throne for a stool and kicking him from it. Hell must have been full of proud men, and the Devil used them for his jailers as Napoleon had done for his penal colonies, which were for the hardest unforgiving men.

'But who will look after them?' his marshals asked.

'Worse men,' the answer.

Henry Stands stopped and stood rigid, and Jude Brown snorted for grain but all Henry did was pass up the reins to me and walk away without a word.

I looked up, afraid as ever when Henry Stands became less than natural, and watched him tread as if the whole ground were bear trapped, and then I saw what he was walking to.

He reached to one of his drawings spiked on a twig, a white bird with a gold hat. I should know better than that but the appreciation of birds is a singular thing to men much as I imagine hats are to women.

Henry held it out in his hands and then moved on. I kicked Jude to follow and I saw that there was another farther on. Henry plucked it carefully from its branch as if it were alive. Even I could see this was a redheaded woodpecker.

He folded these into his coat, and me and Jude were at his shoulder by that time. I began to hear the river ahead and the path opened up and it was me who saw the nest with the blue-brown body atop.

I called him to it and Henry took a knee.

'It is a rails' nest,' he said. 'Breeding early.' He laid the bird aside and sifted through the mess to pick out my father's bullets. 'This has been put here. Shot and carried. Rails will nest in the sedges and cattail.' He looked behind. 'Probably from where we've come.' He stood. 'She could have come from Mexico to get here to this.'

I got down and came to his side. The shattered eggshells and their small occupants and lifeless mother did not bother me unduly but the engine of their demise was everything.

'Why do this, Mister Stands? If they thought us dead . . .'

'They did not find you,' he said. 'I am the one that is dead. It is possible that this is just their spree.'

Children, was my thought. The wanton acts of low minds. 'They are going east, still.'

'For you.' This said as a fact. Henry moved to the stones of the river and scrambled across the rocks for something. He came up with his leather book. He walked back leafing through it.

'Is it badly damaged, Mister Stands?' I said as kindly as I could.

'It is fine.' He put it in its bag.

'Why would they take it?'

'These are men that like to take. Like to take things that others hold. I heard a teamster once took a barrel of cement, which set on the way home. He left it on the road and on the way back in the morning did he not find that some other had picked it up? They will take bolts from wagons that are no use to anyone. They will take the sod off a man's grave.'

He bid me walk the horse over the creek, which had little trickling falls right and left of us. Mister Stands told me that this was a Lehigh creek and that as it went up it had grand waterfalls and trails that were the finest in the land and had been tamed by the coal merchants into canals to carry heat to Philadelphia and New Jersey.

'When you have more time you should get out of New York and come back here. See the falls.'

'Can we not see them now?' I was willing to delay.

He laughed loud, something I had never heard, and Jude Brown's ears raised along with mine.

'That is for you and your girl, son!' he said, and pulled Jude Brown more than let him walk.

Henry Stands's Tanner's atlas was modern enough to show that we were passing through Monroe county, but to most this was still Northampton and Pike borders, and thus the law in Stroud would have to determine just where the crimes against us had been committed. What the map did not show was the Pocono range we would have to go through to get to Stroud, and the only sure road would be the Wilkes-Barre turnpike if we were not to add another day to our task, but mister

Stands decided we should cross the country to avoid the toll. East was our passage, Henry Stands insisted. Keep to it and we would hit Stroud, skirt the mountains and we would sleep the better for it, one more day sleeping and eating in wilderness.

'It is ironic that I can now no longer afford to work. I cannot get to Cherry Hill without a horse.'

I offered thinly from behind, 'You could have Jude Brown. I would owe you that much.' My mother would expect such a sacrifice.

'He is a walking horse.' Henry snorted. I took this as dismissive.

'My only path is to take you to your man in Jersey, get his coin, and purchase anew.'

This pleased me for I still had incertitude that Henry Stands might study his error in escorting me and clear off. I knew when I first saw him that monies would be the way to fashion Henry Stands. I only wished that it had not come to this realization.

There was the impression that we were to abstain from dinner, Henry Stands determined to get out of the beech and maple, and I was disapproving. I had not eaten since supper last and had only tea this morning. Henry Stands's indignation at losing his guns had obviously fueled him beyond food, and walking had obstinated him further. I, however, had almost lost my life to a ghoul and I would dishonor him by enjoying life. Besides, I was a boy and getting a headache from my hunger and that was surely why my hands were shaking also.

Jude Brown had the saddlebags along with the high-back saddle, so privately I snaked my hand backward into the bag for the poke of dodgers.

I bent awkwardly and spilled out of the saddle instead. I hit the ground on my back. I was fortunate not to find rock but I had the breath blown from my lungs.

Henry Stands loomed over me. He was still at first and my instinct was to smile, then he yanked me up by all of me and my skin to his face.

'What are you doing!' he bellowed.

He flung me back to the ground.

'Can you not be good and able for one day!' These were not questions.

He turned away with a hung back and led Jude Brown off with a snap.

I sat up and guessed I was walking from this point, Jude Brown empty of rider. I stayed behind out of both their shadows that I did not deserve.

I measured what we both carried now, Henry Stands and I. But he had done nothing. It was the boy who had ruined everything. The middling wheat ruining this year and the next. I thought on my aunt's plan to place me in that fellow Fellenberg's institution, where the rich boys and the poor boys learned their futures. I put my hands in my pockets as I walked.

There would not be a class for me.

TWENTY-ONE

We were near on the exterior of Jackson by nightfall. There were lots of townships here that profited on the passing lumber and coal companies and Jackson was one of those. By passing companies I mean those of the Lehigh canals and the wagons that supplemented them, for the horse was still the burden bearer over all.

First would come a tract of land purchased by a Smith or a Jones, then a log church by the Friends or the Mennonites. Hotels and mercantiles follow. Then, on the outskirts, where the single men and the drunks that the taverns of the town discourage gather, where the teamsters pass, come the saloons and brothels. Eventually they fall into the townships' quarters but for now, for travelers like Henry Stands and me, they are the rim of the pots of life. And without him speaking of it I knew that the plank building with the plank porch and full rank of four horses tied to its fence was just such a place he was looking for.

'We have no money for bought food,' I said. 'Or drink,' I offered, knowing that Henry Stands would seek spirits. 'We have nothing to trade.'

I did not want to stop here.

'I'm just looking for news,' Henry Stands said, but did not look at me. I could not argue. At that time the inns of the road were the mail drops and polling stations and if you wanted word that is where it was posted. But I think Henry Stands sought something else.

'Wait here,' he said. 'Get up and stay on the horse.'

I watched him sidle away to our left. The saloon was nothing more than a log house with paned windows either side of the stable-door, the top half open, but I could see little of the inside.

I lost sight of mister Stands; he could be Indian when it suited. Me and Jude Brown stood in the dark and I patted his neck and soothed.

It was only moments later when I felt the stout body beside me and Henry Stands laid a hand softly to me so as I would not jump.

'They are here,' he said, and I knew what he meant.

'All of them?'

'All of them,' he said.

'So we go for the law, do we not?' My voice was not as strong as I wanted.

'The law is in Stroud,' he said. 'We are here. I have checked their horses. There are no guns there. They would have them all with them.'

187

I looked up at the light from the saloon. 'So we have nothing to go against them?'

He ignored that and pushed me to take the wooden Paterson from my belt for himself, still stained with tea and ash.

'Take the barrel of the gun to the back door. It is in the corner and covers the room. You will be behind them.'

I stared, and he described the horror further with glee in his voice and the plaything being fondled in his fist.

'Around the back. It is a half door like the front. You will hold over the half like you have a shotgun on them. They will know no better. They will not see you covering them and I will show you when it is right. When I make my play.'

He did not seem to comprehend that our weapons were nothing but toys and broken things and I thought it timely to mention.

'We will be killed!'

He put the steel barrel of his dead wind-rifle in my arms. 'Thomas Walker,' he said, 'have I not shown you cowards? What did I say about Lewis and his rifle?'

Sniffling, I wiped my nose. 'He put fear in the Indians.'

'He put fear in the Indians,' he repeated. 'And if you make a man afraid?'

'You can beat him.'

'You can beat him.' He took my hand but I pulled away. He let me do this and stood aside.

'I may need you here, son,' he said, and waited. I could hear coarse laughter from the saloon. He looked to the soft light. I did not move. He let me sit in silence.

'Stay then,' he said at last, and spat to the dirt. He wiped his foot on it.

'I forget you are a boy.'

He set off toward the light. Invisible at first in the night and then, as he gained upon it, he was a black coat and hat framed against it, smaller than I had ever seen him.

My hands held tight the barrel he had left me and I watched him go on with the fiction of a gun hanging from his right hand.

I may have overdone the fisherman's lure that was Henry Stands's bravery or I may not. The gullible fish snaps at the shine and meat and is whipped from the river to the bank. Even in his last breaths he is unaware that his end has come by just painted wood and wire. He believed it glorious and worthy of the risk.

What you may make of a man approaching abomination with a wooden pistol in his hands is your faith's decision. If you are young I hope it does not inspire too much. I told the same story to my late sons. If you are older you may think Henry Stands foolish, or worse, bitten by madness, or you may yet feel something rising in your chest at the thought of yourself about to stand down four armed men with nothing but your valor and self as your only true weapon. I have given you only a wooden toy.

I did not know what faith Henry Stands had. He said he was a Proverbs man.

They must have been his own proverbs.

I patted Jude Brown, left him, and walked toward the light.

*

'Mister Stands?' My questioning voice was a whisper, the metal tube writhing in my fists. He looked down at me, half his face lit by the glow from the log building. He instructed over the doubt in my words.

'To the back,' he said. 'You will see the door. It is open. Wait for my call on it. When you hear me, stand up. They will be looking on me.' That was all he said and carried on his slow path and did not look over to see if I was going on.

I had the empty steel. I had Thomas Heywood encased in a room and armed with my father's guns. I could hear his raucous laughter as I crept to the back door. He was roaring over my destitution, my orphan position of his making. He had triumphed over Henry Stands and the orphan was surely dead. He was safe in this place. Safe with his partners and the rum bought with my father's guns and coin. Safe as any man in his coffin and I looked down at what I had against him and thought of Henry Stands coming through the front door with the model of a gun, and I did not want to think further. But I would keep my faith.

Their laughter was loud now and as if aimed at me, as if they could see through the walls and watched and mocked my fool's approach. The top half of the door was swung outward and showed the shadows of them, the heads of them stretched and warped as the stove-light played. I heard the flap of cards and the friendly curses of rum and villainy. No music or the sense of others, just the flat echoes of an expansive room.

And then I had no time for fear as I heard the front door open slow and a new shadow rose on the wood above my head.

There was the sound of chairs scraping and glass dancing but then Henry Stands's voice silenced it all.

'Easy there, boys,' he said. 'I'll shoot if you ain't respectful.'

I stood up now, and what a picture I saw!

There were only two tables and these were sorry poor, as was the whole, which was not much more than a barn.

The bar was a bookcase with a blanket tacked across its front and another bookcase on the wall behind with crock and glass bottles. There was a vegetable box for spitting.

The tramp of a barkeep was ducked and looking at Henry Stands in the door. I had all the backs to me, all standing, and it was just them backs of the four who had changed my life, the place empty save for them. I saw two rifles propped under the bar.

This was the whole world.

I saw Henry Stands pass the wooden pistol over them, keeping it at his waist.

The light was low, just the stove and one lamp above the table where their game was waiting. Everything just shapes like puzzle pieces, all half-lit, and Henry Stands had plotted well. He had the shape of a gun pointed at them. And he could read their thinking.

'The boy at the door.' He raised his left hand slow to indicate.

Indian-hatband turned his head and saw me with my steel ready to paint their backs and I made my face hateful as best I could. He made a whisper to Heywood.

Heywood lifted his hands away from his belt. I could see that the saw-toothed blanket he wore as a coat was

191

crudely cut up the back for when he rode. He cared nothing for what he looked like. If he lay asleep you would pass him by for a pile of rags.

'You got the drop, old-timer,' he said, and raised himself up. 'What you want?'

I thrilled! Had we done it?

I brandished my gun like a lookout with an eight-gauge in a city bar.

Had we done it?

'I want you to drop your belts and irons, boys,' Henry Stands said. 'I want only my goods back and what is left of the boy's. The law is on you, so good luck to you. I don't hold that against, but you took from me. And I cannot stand for that.'

Damn if I could still not see the face of that man who was just black coat and hat! He moved a step away from the others and Henry Stands moved with him with just wood to threaten.

'Hold there,' Henry said to Black-coat's twitching. 'You'll go first.'

He called to me.

'Boy? Shoot Heywood's back. I'll nail this son of a bitch.'

And I lifted that empty barrel to my underarm, making to fire! Hatband saw and gritted his teeth at Heywood.

'N-now hold there!' Heywood stammered, and lifted his arms higher. 'Ain't no reason to go, old friend! We can talk this out.'

Henry lowered the gun.

'You keep calling me "old," you wet bastard.' He set his feet apart with the wooden gun by his thigh. 'Drop.

That's the end of it. You can drink on and I'll be gone with them pistols. Keep your own.'

I saw Heywood's head tilt in thought and the scene was as a painting, not a finger moving.

'My boys said you were dead?' He said this to himself.

'Lot of folks tell that.'

Heywood moved one pace.

'Where'd you get that gun, old man?' There was backbone in his voice. 'We cleaned you out. That's one of the boy's pistols . . .?'

He swung his head to me and his eyes were black like Strother Gore's.

'Where'd you get any gun, come to think . . .'

I began to shiver within and Heywood smiled.

Henry brought him back.

'Damn if I don't have friends,' he said, and moved to the bar. Black-coat shifted with him and Henry lifted the gun just enough. Black-coat's boots stayed at that.

'You may not know that word, son,' Henry said kindly. 'My man Irish. Back on the road. Friend of mine. You sold him our property. I went back to my friend. I stand with his guns. Right pleased he was to understand what a fool you made of him. The road's closed to you boys now.'

Heywood's hands lowered.

'I don't think so,' he said. 'I don't think you've done that. I think, old man, that you're standing there with the wooden piece we left with the boy . . . I think that's the measure of it . . .'

Henry Stands turned his wooden gun to the barkeep.

'They sell you them stolen guns for their drink?'

I could not see the man for he had shrunk below his

bar, and then I stopped looking, for the four went for their belts, slow, or I recall it as slow, but they never concerned themselves with me, and if I was truly armed that would have been their last mistake.

The scrape of leather, my father's guns, the table heaved over for a shield, glass and cards flying.

I never saw Henry Stands drop behind the bar, only the twin barrels of the shotgun that came up with him. Providence! You go try and find a barkeep who does not have such at his knee!

He brought up the gun, as they say when you shoot bird, and calmly, like shooting the same, planted his aim. No care for the iron at him. This was his measure. I could see him draw and hold breath.

The others fired loose, as if afraid of their guns, and they huddled together as they shot wildly like at the fluttering of bats. They were back-shooters not shootists. Counterfeits all their lives.

Henry Stands sewed them with the shotgun's sight. One closed eye and a pull and Indian-hatband's face exploded to the wall mid-giggle and his teeth rattled on the floor still laughing. Henry swung left, never minding the bottles blowing out behind him, and Black-coat cocked but nothing else, as his head painted the window and his legs danced him to the corner. He brought the other table down and it covered him and I never did see what he truly looked like.

Just Heywood and Silver-hair now. Heywood was near on his back, pushing himself to the wall and palming back the Colt but playing it high. Three shots he had done, all above Henry's head, and Henry went below the bar again.

Silver-hair had got back his sense. He had one of the revolvers also and went to a knee for the rest of his shots.

I drew the bolt of the door and came in running. Two steps and I was on him.

I swung that Italian steel and cleaved it into Silver-hair's head like an ax. It stuck, which I did not expect, and I let go, a horrible shiver up my arm. It carried with him as he keeled over and I could do nothing but stare as it stood out of the back of his head like a candle. My eyes ran to the Colt quivering in his fist and I dove on it.

Prying it from that hand was the first time I had it placed for real. I had known its press into my belly when my father had clasped me that night in Milton and when I had shown Henry how to load it, and the wooden grip was the same in my hand as the model. But now it was a weapon. I had a pistol in my hand. And nothing feels the same as that. It has a beauty to it for sure. Like it was meant to be. You understand that or you do not.

Thomas Heywood was at the back wall, legs spread, his chest panting. He looked to his dead and cocked the Colt again. Silence then.

There had been Henry Stands's two shotgun blows and the repeat of the Colts, their white smoke turning in the air and hanging under the stove's blue, but now no sound but the dying breath of men and the roll of bottles across the planked floor.

Heywood saw the pistol in my hand and shakily leveled his own to me. Mister Colt's craftsmanship now destined to be the tool of the slovenly saloon brigand.

195

Colt spoke of army and navy contracts, of the defense of the homesteader.

I would tell him what the future of his guns was to be.

He would not be able to hear his own verbiage over the epochal horror of the repeating gun.

I mirrored Heywood, he who had my name, and my gun came up less shaky than his. Double-handed I pulled the hammer back, felt the parts within tense in my fist, saw the percussion cap waiting; then a shot came from the bar and put Heywood down.

The first Colt in Henry's outstretched arm. Small bore for a saddle but fine from across a stinking tavern. I did not fire.

Henry Stands came from the bar with the Colt smoking. I guess they had sold that rotten barkeep one as Henry Stands had supposed.

In his left hand he had taken up the wooden model again. He stepped across the room as Heywood patted at his wound, spluttered his blood, and lifted his gun arm.

Henry Stands came slowly on. He lifted the wooden pistol and cocked and fired its empty flat noise at Heywood and then followed it with the real, which pinned Heywood's shoulder to the wall. This was his gun arm, now dead, but still he tried to lift it as he fell to his bones.

The wooden gun at him again, fired duly again, and Thomas Heywood choked and coughed blood on the amusement of it. But Henry Stands was not yet done.

He rolled his fist and fired the steel Paterson again and the crack of it shook the walls and Henry walked

196

through the smoke so that it trailed behind and he clicked the wooden one once more at Heywood. Then again the real as Heywood slipped farther, and again the wood, and again the real straight after, and the sickening thud of lead into carcass stays with me still.

He had a pattern now.

The gun loosed from Heywood's hand, trickled to the floor, and he looked up to Henry Stands. I could not see Henry's face. He cocked and pointed the wooden pistol and fired its empty promise at Heywood's head.

The dying trash grinned and found the strength to pull Henry's skinning knife from his belt. He waved it weakly, his arm crooked like a dog's paw, and he whimpered like the same.

Henry fired into Heywood's blood mouth and I shut my eyes at the sight. The last shot.

I opened them at the sound of Henry's boots. He picked up a bottle from the floor and drained it high down his throat. I noticed only then that he still had his hair tied in the bow I had made.

The barkeep drew himself up and Henry did not take the bottle from his mouth but raised the wooden gun to him and the barkeep went back below. I looked to the wall. A good third of it red from all of them, hair mixed with splinters of wood. It would never paint over. Years later the town decreed to take it out and build another to stop people coming to see it.

Blood from Silver-hair's head ran to my boot and I looked down at it and the gun in my hand. I stepped away. I had shot nothing. Thomas Heywood's body was crumpled on his side like he had no ribs.

I minded the blood less than I thought I would have.

How I felt about that saloon would come much later. I had killed a man and had been ready to shoot another, but I could not think on that now. When these things occur you will surprise yourself how gathered you can be. Or I was now tainted and familiar.

Henry Stands went to the bar, left the dead behind him, and planted the bottle and called up the keep.

If that skulker had a voice Henry did not care.

'You. Get up here.' He drank again as the bony fellow crept up. 'Any trappings these gentlemen have is yours. Save for the guns they took from me and the boy. They sold you a pistol that was not theirs so I must confiscate or you can give me rum for it. I'll take one of their horses too. They killed a good horse of mine. I ain't no thief.' He tipped his old headpiece. 'My thanks for keeping your mistress loaded.'

He turned back and stomped to me. He did not even look at Silver-hair. 'Trade,' he said, and took the Colt from my hand and passed me the model. 'Go choose a horse and find my belt. I'll clear up.'

'They might have my Dutch oven!'

'Well, that was my motivation.' He had already begun to forage about their bodies.

Outside I found Henry's belt, which still had his long knife on it, and chose a good pale quarter horse who I was sure would be grateful to have some good company for a change.

Looking out I could just make Jude Brown waiting where I left him. He had not come in to see the others and he had not ducked and run at the shooting. I guess he knew we were making good on the friend he had in Henry's horse. And I would make good on him when

I got home. He would be the best-fed horse in New York city. And was not I going home now? No forks in my road?

I stood and waited with the horse, my thoughts on my father as the horse breathed beside my ear and I could feel the warmth from him. How many days? Still April? I would have to think on that. The men who had put my father early to the earth now dead themselves by a man who had never seen him or known why he should have put them down for taking the good John Walker from raising his son proper. And who would do that now? There would be more mister Markhams in my future or that institutional schooling that my aunt had studied. I thought the death of Heywood would be the end of it and I would be as right as the mail from now on. But going home would be the end and the beginning.

Henry came out. He did not say it but I think he admired the horse.

'Bring him along,' he said. 'They did not have my Harper's pistols. They break one miracle and trade another. Got my skinning knife back.'

'And the Patersons?' I asked.

'Five of them,' he said. He must have had them in his pockets and tucked about. 'I gave one for rum. You won't mind that?'

'Well.' I followed. 'You had no right. And you have made a mess of that man's business even if you have left him three horses and thieves' coin. But I suppose the law can clear that up satisfactorily.'

Henry Stands twisted on his heel and angled at me. I hoped in the dark he could see my smile.

'I made a joke, Mister Stands,' I said.

'Good for you.' He snorted. He flicked a finger at me. 'You got blood on your face.' He wiped his own to show me where. 'Better that than you crying them tears all the time as you do.'

He turned and walked on and I wiped my cheeks and pulled the horse after us.

Behold – I have smitten my hand at thy dishonest gain which thou hast made, and at thy blood which has been in the midst of thee.

Ezekiel 22: 12–13.

TWENTY-TWO

'Shaws, McDowells, and Brodheads. God knows what else resides around here.' Henry Stands was happy and fat next morning. He lolled on his new horse like a king and we had eaten the steak of his other for breakfast. He was already at his rum and singing his songs, the night before not apparent. I can only think back on Chet Baker's words when describing the man:

'He likes the sound of guns.'

We were coming into Stroud, the road muddy and wide, and I recognized that I had come through here with my father but it had been almost night then and we rode on through and camped. I did not question at that time why we did not rest here but Henry Stands made sense of my late father's reasoning.

'Two Friends' meetinghouses. Presbyterian church, Methodist, and the Free. They even have a temperance hotel. A man will die of thirst and sleep cold at night in such a place.'

They would not have appreciated a salesman of guns. But I knew civilization when I saw it.

Daniel Stroud had sold plots when his father, Jacob, who had founded this place, would not, but he sold them on condition that the houses were built away from the road with yards in front and behind and proper fences and planked walkways.

Trees lined the streets, and families walked among them. Canes and stovepipes for the men, and bonnet hats with exotic feathers for the ladies. Henry Stands pointed at the ladies' hats, for which vulgarity they shunned him with their parasols.

'They wear Carolina parrakeet tails in their hatbands. That bird is almost dead for vanity. People are infinite, creatures are not.' He tipped his hat at their scowls and their husbands' frowns. I did the same and enjoyed their bluster. We did not have a carriage so we were low to them. They had forgotten that their town was built by lumber and sweat.

There was no love for men and company in Henry Stands and I am sure the bricks and proper houses had already begun to stiffen his stance in the poor saddle he had inherited. He had left me with his more comfortable rigging on Jude Brown, which my hind was grateful for.

There could have been no decency to us. We slept in the open and wore it on us. I did not care. My clothes were not me. I lived in a redbrick house on sett streets. These folks walked on planks like sailors.

Stroud was the county seat since the year last. She had sawmills and a grist mill, a tannery, and along her river a large iron forge. She was prosperous even in those hard times and had sunk many a settlement around her to become *the* town after the Delaware. Where her academy stood had been a fort and she had once boasted two, and it was to Stroud where the settlers had fled after the Wyoming massacre. But I remembered Henry Stands's pose on that. When settlers are victorious it is recorded as a battle. When Indians triumph it is a 'massacre.' And we do not write so much that there were four hundred loyalist Tory rangers at that killing, plugging at white folks. Some of those scowlers sneering at our hooves were descended from that ilk no doubt.

We pulled up at Hollinshead's tavern, opposite one of Jacob Stroud's original houses in the center of the town. We both dismounted and stood still and looked at each other. You may think this ordinary but when you are on the road it is in single file. When you stand it is for food and discourse and important things.

'There is law here,' Henry said. He checked both our trappings. 'What do you want to do?'

This was the only time I remember this man asking my opinion. He stood over his horse, us both sullying the gaily lit afternoon with our weary coats.

'What am I to do?'

'Did you not want the law?' he said. 'Tell your story?' He rubbed his beard. 'I could break. There are folks here that will see you home.'

I watched carriages with padded seats and glass roll

past, black broughams and landaus. I had not seen prosperity for a while.

'Mister Stands? I must pay you for my trouble from my orders. There is Mister Colt's monies owed through my father's order book. Paterson is not so far for you to make your way to Philadelphia.'

He stretched his back and stamped his boots, his eyes on the colorful tavern. 'They have oysters and beer here. And seats. When was the last time you sat well?'

'I thought we had no coin for refreshments? I do not think they will trade for guns?' I had done for the Colts now. I would put them in the Delaware.

'*You* have no coin,' Henry said, and went to his purse among his folds and flashed me Mexican silver. 'I have means, and you should know beer and oysters.'

'I thought we had nothing? You sold powder to that Irishman?'

'Trade is trade. You get less for coin. You will find this. Especially when the country is in hell.' He had already mounted the porch of the hotel. 'You should know what a beer tastes like after days on the road. All is to the good. You have nothing to fear now.'

He was right. The road behind me was closed. A door bolted from my side. Only my own front door ahead of me. Oh, there would be a terrible day to tell to my aunt, but within my own walls I could stop to think, to rest, to judge. But still I wanted this man beside me. I had to confront mister Colt with my sorry platter and an order book with pages that had been strewn about the wilds and tucked back in. I would need a man of consequence.

I tied the horses as he watched and then stamped up

the plank steps to join him, then in a flash spun back to my folded blanket behind the saddle to retrieve the tea-stained wooden gun.

Henry Stands waited in the doorway.

'I thought you wanted to burn that thing?'

I said nothing and tucked it behind my back beneath my coat and ran under his arm.

As a boy I did not retain my Bible. I look through it now and see more and more of what was me then and much that is of me now. Any man's whole life is there.

When I meet a man who does not have faith in anything other than himself I would be as dumb as him to pity or try to change him. They have great pride, I will give them that. They congratulate themselves for when things go well but are the most likely ones you will find hanging in their barns when things go against. I find that these men do not understand the companionship of animals either. I think of words now. Words that fill me with memories and hope.

> *I have told you these things, so that in me you may*
> *have peace.*
> *In this world you will have trouble.*
> *But take heart! I have overcome the world!*

There are those of us who in recent years have turned to look on the battlefield to see our hopes, our dearly loved children, swept away. We do not hang ourselves in our grief. We rise and bear, and you can mark us from those cowards and counterfeiters well enough:

We have a Bible in our homes.

And though our boughs can be cut by Heaven I never saw a tree that was ever completely destroyed by lightning.

TWENTY-THREE

The beer was a dark porter, with the yeast still on top, it seemed. Mrs Hollinshead herself made up our oysters, which I had to go and collect at the bar. We had to line up with the guests and the travelers and give our order and then wait to be called. It was a smart establishment and fitted out with a high ceiling and mahogany paneling all about. There was a post-table set against a wall even though I had seen a post office and Stroud had a Posten stage that delivered passengers and mail from Easton twice daily. But the post-tables were what folks still expected. Here a lone traveler could pick up a letter that was going someplace on his road and take it with him. He could expect a small meal for his trouble and maybe make a friend or two. People got to hear news and changes from the road even if it was only about the cut of dresses in the east and the politics of the original colonies that made no difference to any of us. But the government was making no money out of that so we got post offices instead of friends. And no government ever did like to have no control over news or the exchange of opinions.

When a man is on the road to power he buys everyone a drink. Once elected he tries to close the saloons.

I had never had oysters before, what with them being a poor food, but baked they were not disagreeable. Beer I had drunk many a time but not as strong, and I understood the word *heady* after I was only halfway through my pewter.

Henry Stands's eyes twinkled at my foolish grin over my mug. He rubbed his nose and cleared his throat as he often did when he was about to say something I disliked.

'Now, son, the way I see it, we can put you to a judge here and see what he has to say. Tell it as it is. Nothing to hide.'

I put my head close to the table and whispered, 'But did we not . . . kill men?'

'Self-defense. We are not vigilantes or desperadoes.' He glared at me 'Do our acts concern you?'

I sat back. I had slept on it, breakfasted over it, and now chewed on my dinner, and although my hands at the time had trembled I felt no God bearing down on me.

'It happened very naturally,' I said. 'You gave them fair play.'

'It was an even-break. They died in their boots,' he said.

You may misunderstand this phrase, think it noble. It is of fiction. Good men die in their bed with their boots off. There were times when 'boots on' has been enough to acquit a man of murder.

'Can you not take me back, Mister Stands? Just to Paterson? I would not like to lose out on meeting with Mister Colt.'

He looked around the room, measured the rest of our companions, and ended on Mrs Hollinshead behind the counter.

'I hope she is not a widow,' he said, and then scratched his head before putting his hat on. 'I will take you home. There is the money from your man Colt to appraise. But an incident has occurred. That should be given up. There is your troubles and its resolution and I have some good reputation and standing for honesty.'

'Will the law not take hold of me?'

'I do not suppose. First we should remove my rigging from your horse and then see about it.'

This was a giveaway!

'You are planning to leave me again!'

'Finish your beer. I am to no such thing,' he said. 'No, I am beginning to think that I will be at your wedding and funeral and wipe your behind for both.' He stood. 'I will ask that petulant ring-seeker at the bar where to find a judge.'

He went to the bar, to the middle of it, and set his hands to look like he was holding it up and that he owned the place, as always he stood. He was talking to a man in a cap who had made room for him, a diminu- tive fellow with a bugle on a gold cord at his hip. They went back and forth for a while as I drank my beer.

Henry Stands gave him his 'much obliged' nod when the fellow handed over a letter to him. He came back to me.

'That man. Dean. He is the post-carrier here. He says that Stodgell Stokes is the post office, general store, and judge here. He has a letter for him so we should introduce ourselves.' He walked, and our bright dinner of oysters and beer was solemnly over. I slouched out after him. The small man with the bugle saluted his cap at me. I saw that he had silver hair under that cap and something crawled through me. I did not smile back.

We changed the rigging. The tavern had a livery attached but we had money only for hay. As the horses ate Henry spent a time smartening up his clothes with horse brushes. He was planning to ditch me to a judge, I was sure, but he ignored my sullen face. I knew that we had to make some word to the law but I would rather it had been in a letter or from a distance. I still had my father's work to do.

The tavern was at the end of the main street called Elizabeth, named after one of Stroud's daughters, and with directions from the hostler we rode up to the post office and general store, which was also the judge's trade.

There were some fine manse houses on that street and these were old Stroud homes. That was for certain a family that had done well, but being among palaces is no assurance of good men.

The jolly sound of the bell over the door brought the man in apron and pince-nez beaming toward us from around his counter.

He wiped his hands on a cloth in his apron band,

which he tied at his front. He had those cuff protectors the same as Chet Baker and I liked him right away.

Henry Stands was leaning on the wrists of the Patersons and looking around as patriarchal as ever. He did not remove his hat, so I did for the both of us.

This man, Stodgell Stokes, was about as old as my father and just as clean-shaven.

'Can I assist you, sirs?' He did not mind Henry's guns and winked at me bashfully.

'Are you the judge?' Henry Stands dispensed with the man's other hats.

'I am Judge Stokes, sir.'

'Then I have a letter for your post office, Judge.' Henry put over the letter. 'And I have circumstances. Regarding the boy here.' He threw a shoulder at me. 'Matters of the law.'

Stodgell Stokes kept his office in his residence. He locked his store and we followed him up his narrow stairs.

The paint on Stroud's courthouse was still wet. It had not been the county seat for long. If Judge Stokes was also the post office and the general store I was sure that would not be the case much longer and he would have to make a full-time profession of the law. We were bringing him something weighty and others soon enough would do the same beyond the remit of horse-thieves and stolen toile. Once a town builds a courthouse all manner of evil descends. It is worse than building a brothel.

He bid us to sit before him. Henry Stands flapped out his coat over the arms of his chair and still did not remove his hat.

'Now what is it I can do for you, gentlemen?' Stodgell Stokes was still the storekeeper.

Henry cocked his thumb to me. 'This here is Thomas Walker. He is a boy from New York city. Six nights ago his father was killed on the road. Near Milton.'

'Outside Lewis,' I said. 'In the forest.'

Henry continued for me. My word still a boy's.

'My name is Henry Stands. Orange county. I am a trader. Indiana ranger befores. I am on my way to Cherry Hill to reconnoiter escapees. I am taking the boy home.'

Judge Stokes appeared before us, the nail-seller now put away to a drawer. 'I am sorry to hear this, son. We shall make this a matter for the marshals. I assure you I will make it my strictest priority.' He reached for stylus and paper hidden among cotton reels and a box of pins.

I folded my arms. 'There is no need for marshals, Your Honor. The matter has been settled.'

'Settled?' He blinked at us in turn. 'I'm afraid I do not understand?'

Henry Stands stared through him.

'There were four men that killed the boy's father. They sought to kill the boy. I . . . protected. They robbed him, and us both when they come found us again. I had to settle for them. In self-defense and in defense of the boy.'

The judge sat back, still looking between us.

'Well, of course you did.' He pointed his writing hand to Henry's belt. 'Your pistols there, Mister Stands? With your scabbards as they are, the hilts out. Is that not what one might call a "cavalry draw" . . . sir?'

Henry Stands had placed two of the Patersons in his

old belt. Full-load. There was a pause and I could hear carriages strutting past from the street below.

'It is good for shooting from a horse,' he said.

'Do you shoot from a horse often, Mister Stands?'

Henry offered nothing. Stodgell Stokes waved away the remark. 'No matter. I was only curious. Now these men that killed the poor boy's father. You know them?'

I cut in. Spoke amid men.

'Thomas Heywood!' I declared. 'It was him that did it all!'

Henry Stands put his hand across my front to hush me.

'These were road-agents,' he said. 'They may have been late of Murrell's men traveling east or some such gang. I will not seek reward for doing what is right.'

'You have killed these men?'

Henry Stands held the judge's eye.

You did not ask actual badmen such.

The counterfeit, the imitation, the 'boot-black long-hair' would boast, would tell all. Not in this room.

A hard face from the actual was enough.

Judge Stokes looked away to slice open the letter we had brought to distract himself from that cold look. I think Henry Stands was vying the man and measuring him by the store beneath our feet and I was getting to that opinion also. A man who fancied the law and sold tinware would not know what our road had been like. But then, this man was still a judge despite his apron.

'What is it that you want of the law here, gentlemen?' he said, his spectacles fixed to the page. Them frames were a good six dollars' worth.

Henry Stands shifted.

'About ten miles west there is a tavern. Jackson way.

They are there with three horses. The keep there will be reporting. I do the same. I am taking the boy back to his family. Self-defense is my statement. I took a horse because they killed my own and I had need to escort the boy.' He rubbed his nose. 'That is probably all.'

I leaned to Henry to remind with a whisper about the ghoul Strother Gore but he whisted me back.

A clock chimed off behind us and I jerked but Henry Stands did not stir. His head hung a little as he studied his hands. Stodgell Stokes was reading down his page; he had lost interest in our statement and his eyes flicked to me from over the letter.

'Well,' he said at last. 'I would say that you have done the right thing, Mister Stands, by bringing this to the law. You are to be commended.'

He put back his chair but stumbled as he went up and had to grab for the desk.

'If you will excuse me for but a moment this letter you have brought has determined my immediate attention.' He patted the air to keep us to our seats and took the letter with him.

'I will be a short time, gentlemen.' He shuffled out.

When I had heard him creak down the stairs and that friendly front bell chime, I stood up and leaned on his desk.

'Why should we not tell about that Mister Gore?' I asked.

Henry did not look up from his hands. 'It would do no good. And probably worse.'

'But he had bodies there! There could be good people looking for their relatives?'

216

'As I said. Probably worse.'

This was not a satisfactory answer but I did not press, for that never went well with him.

I looked down at the packet that had carried Stodgell Stokes's letter. It was marked from Berwick. With no thought or malevolence it was in my fingers. I turned it over. The effeminate hand on the back froze my fingers pale.

It was from mister William Markham! Him with boys and asylums on his mind!

Twice a day that stage came into Stroud and mister Markham for all his paunch had a fast pen over his slow feet, I knew that much.

A letter as fast as us!

Judge Stokes had looked at me as he read it and had caught the table as he stood. I was too worn to be taken in by coincidence. I held it up.

'Mister Stands!' I waved the paper. 'His letter is from Mister Markham! That man at Mrs Carteret's!'

I could feel stone walls closing in on the orphan.

Henry stood and took the packet. He looked it over, back and front as if there would be some hidden cipher.

'Son of a bitch,' he said, crushing it and putting it to the floor. 'Should have burst that fat man. God knows what he has written against.'

He took my hand and I planted my hat.

Stodgell Stokes would have slowed us some if he had locked his door. He must have been too trembling to do so.

Outside was a bright spring afternoon, but the street,

217

which had been bustling, was now still. Henry kept a hand to my chest and edged me behind him.

The tall hats and parasols had gone. Instead there were five wide hat-brims and shotguns standing on the planks and mud across the street. Stodgell Stokes both apart and with them. He demonstrated himself too far to be a threat but his voice was veritable enough for an unarmed man.

'You are Henry Stands?' he called, and Henry said nothing and to Stodgell that was enough affirmation for the shotguns.

'Stands, I have a letter from Mister William Markham! Respected member of our church and elected member of our county. He informs that you have kidnapped this boy for reward or to sell into servitude. He states that you are a member of the actual gang that deprived this boy's father of his life and are a wanted roadman that drew a weapon on him and that there are a number of crimes on warrant that are fitted to your description.' He lifted the letter aloft. 'What say you on these charges?'

Those five shotguns were brought up like morning plows as if Henry were the horse and drawing them.

'What you have is incorrect,' Henry said. 'Ask the boy.'

But they did not hear or would not ask. Stodgell Stokes went on.

'The letter states that you have bewildered, seduced, and confused the boy. Do you deny that he is the property of the St John's asylum? Against Mister Markham's word? Kidnapping is a hanging, sir!'

I could feel the air crisp. These lies, these paper lies, which are the worst and shape wars, were making the round world into a square.

I would shape it back.

I stepped in front of Henry Stands, my arms spread. 'No! This man is taking me home! I have agreed to all!'

Some flat-brimmed hat yelled over to me from behind his breech.

'Stand aside, boy! You are safe now!'

Another cocked his piece. 'The Hoosier has the boy hostage!'

That snapped them all into life.

Henry Stands stood solid. Prey and predator, but I would remain his shield.

My father had made me the same in front of him and I told you I have made peace with that. I should have volunteered then. I volunteered now because I knew death. It has nothing to do with fear. Fear only precipitates. And perhaps I might have saved my father still if I had not just sat on the ground that night and watched.

I stood in front now, like I should have done before, against five guns at my body. To save all three of us. My father watching.

'He is my friend!' I yelled.

'Away, boy!' This came from a black coat and hat. His face hidden behind his gun, high collar, and pulled-down brim. I had seen that shadow. It was now a common shape to me. I think that is how the Devil walks the earth.

Henry Stands edged me aside. I looked at his black fingernails on my chest.

'Get,' he said.

I never heard his voice again.

He stepped down to his horse as if the guns were not there and they stood transfixed on him. He pulled his huge knife and cut the rein and was up on him in the same move.

He dug his knees to put that quarter horse into the middle of the street. Those gentlemen stepped back with their shotguns high, and Stodgell Stokes ducked behind a barrel with his liar's letter.

The black coat was the first to set his gun.

This was not right! We had eaten oysters and beer, we had come to the law, we had destroyed enemies. I was to home! This was happening too fast, too unfair!

Henry Stands threw down on the guns against him. That elitist cross-draw that was bespoke to the ranger. Two pistols in his fists. A crowd of guns stepped from the plank walk but they were not soldiers, they were not rangers. And they did not have Colt's 'Improved Revolving Gun.'

That quarter horse was an outlaw's so I guess he had some knowledge and resistance of gunfire or Henry Stands squeezed him tight enough. He wheeled once and gave one shot from each hand to the windows over the nearest shotguns' heads.

The shotguns ducked but felt confident now that he had spent his hands. Two of them fired, but to the sky. Counterfeits think that one barrel high is enough to stop, that no man is used to that sound opposing him.

Only the black coat stepped from the planks and let both his barrels go, and straight on, but that meant nothing to Henry Stands. He stared into the fire as it came. It is hard to shoot a man, no matter how black your coat, and harder still when the man in front dares it.

They all thought him done. An old man with two

pistols spent. But Henry Stands would show them the future.

He rolled those Colts in his fists and slammed lead into their painted houses. They cut back in their surprise. Still those shots came on.

It was a wonder now. Unseen anywhere! Unending! There was not a man ever before who carried two pistols and sent shotguns running as he fired repeatedly, fired magically!

Eight shots in the hand, from the saddle, again and again. They ran like the first animals from the first fire.

The street emptied. Henry and his horse whirled in the white smoke, his quarter horse's head set west. I had not ducked. I had no doubts.

He put the pistols to his scabbards and took back the short rein. His head looked round for guns, to eat them if they still stood, but they had cowered to behind their doors. He had killed none. That was not his intention.

I saw his coat sweep and that quarter horse fly, the mud barely leaping. Hands grabbed to stop me from running to the street.

He was gone.

I write those words like I had a patent.

EPILOGUE

Mister William Markham was true to his word. He had sent one letter of destruction sure enough, but his fervent pen had stretched to New York also, which was as well, for if not I had been set to spend some time in a house of stone and oak where boys are apt to be forgotten.

The court had found my aunt and my aunt had sent for me while Stodgell Stokes waited to find some soul willing to take a boy to the asylum in Allegheny. There had naturally been a reluctance due to my recent history, despite a twenty-dollar bounty waiting on me for the purveyor.

There might, after all, be a grizzled old man with fire in his fists on the road.

I returned to New York and my aunt's sorrow, with

a bill for my return and keep. Her loss was great and we bore it together with me patting her shoulder as I imagined.

I showed her the wooden gun and my father's book and told her that I had to get to Paterson and to mister Colt for my father's money that I owed to Henry Stands.

It was strange to talk about him to someone who did not know him and when everything surrounding him seemed wrong. My words not eloquent enough to get across to Aunt Mary how very important it was that we find the man. I did not cry anymore, but maybe that would have helped my insistence.

In truth, between the wooden thing, which I kept under my bed, and the settling of mister Colt, the finding of Henry Stands was the only thing.

My aunt decided that to write to mister Colt would be enough.

You may know that Sam Colt was notorious for not paying his bills. The revolving gun was not a resounding success at that time. We never got any coin and would have to have stood in a long line to do so.

His business was wound up in '42. He wrote us a poorly scripted letter citing that because my father could not return any of the samples, Henry Stands having made off with five and Heywood trading the rest, and the orders amounted to but one hundred and twenty-nine dollars, which he would follow up on, of course, our commission had been swallowed by the loss of the guns. He included a bill for the difference, which I burned.

I married young, as was the expectation in those days.

I took my wife, Mary, in the same year my aunt and Jude Brown died. Mary seemed an inevitable name for me to find. She was an orphan also but had her own seamstress shop and did not need to marry a spectacle salesman.

I sold the house on Bank street (I told you I knew it) and moved to Lycoming when Mary's belly swelled. New York is no place for a family if you can afford to avoid it.

I wanted to settle somewhere near the Susquehanna, and I took her to see the Lehigh falls on the way. We bought our place outright with enough land to feed ourselves; no government would catch me. Pigs, one cow, chickens, and a plow. Neighbors for the rest. That is how it should be. Yet I owe, as do you, as I said. It happens. Banks gun for you eventually, especially once you have family. Sometimes you envy them drifters.

We named our first son John Walker.

I had some insurance from my father's death and I did indeed sell spectacles by mail using my father's suppliers. I decided not to sell guns.

Married, and with my sales, I could map the prosperity of the states by their orders, almost to their streets, and I settled on Old Lycoming as a town where I would set up an optometrist store. I had become my own Chet Baker!

All of that was in the first year of John's life, and our second son came right along behind him.

We named him Henry.

I wrote to mister Chet Baker in Milton that I would like to hear word of Henry Stands if he came across it, and bless that man if he did not write back to say that he would forward my details to every salesman and traveler who came by him.

Chet and I kept letters until '70, when a stroke took him. He outlived my sons. His store is now split in two as a barber and confectionary. Nothing of Henry Stands ever came through.

The revolving gun did spread, particularly down in Texas with the settlers and the rangers, and I knew why for that. It was an adept killing tool for one man against the many. I am sure Colt envisioned that when the Devil mothered his invention.

From time to time word of its peculiar success made the papers. He had made enough of them and they found their way into the best and worst hands.

In New York, as I grew to manhood, Colt's patents were being made under license. Six shots now. We had fallen for the revolver. Fallen far. You know the names that made it famous but I balked when I read about the Colt Walker, which made such an impact in the Mexican war of '48. Fortunately it was just coincidence but I sagely acknowledged the Comanche saying that came up from those lands:

White man shoots one time with rifle. And six times with butcher knife.

By then I was in Old Lycoming with two children at my knee. I had put my past behind me and was known as a man of still countenance and quiet strength. I never had a bill that was not settled.

My wife Mary and myself were good Mennonites, her religion not mine; I was a Proverbs man. I thought no more on guns and Indiana rangers until my boys were old enough for me to tell them about the wooden gun and I went to my past to fetch it.

I could not find it.

I searched through our barn with all the goods that young marrieds always store and there were song sheets and shawls and pepper grinders and coffee jars and even puppets and dolls that Mary had carried with her all her days. There were paper brooches and letters from Chet Baker and wooden toys that held no memory but no flared pistol grip of two pieces and engraved wooden cylinder. Mary questioned if I had not imagined such a piece.

I cursed and shouted and went to bed drunk and Mary cried for the first time. I apologized the next day.

I told her about Strother Gore and that I had killed a man with an extraordinary blow, the story of which I had never told even to my aunt. I blamed that tale on the reason for my temper. She knew about Henry Stands, of course, for I had used that story to woo her, but I had kept back the darker parts.

Still the wooden gun was lost. Spirited away when I had stopped holding it and thinking of it. When I did not have need for it.

I am sure I had it with me when I left New York but my hands were full at the time. Things get lost when you make a family and a home. But I had it within me and I told the story to my sons, and drew the wooden Paterson for them, and told them about Henry Stands as I have now fully told you.

*

My sons died in Columbus in '65. The spring of the end. I told them the day they volunteered to find a ranger and stick by him and pay no mind to West Point boys. John was nineteen and Henry eighteen. That was eight years ago. I have a letter from Sherman commending them.

We have the metal cartridge now, the complete round, and Colt's rear-loading pistols. He has found favor again. The glorious terms *Peacemaker* and *Frontier* and the self-loading rifle are shaping the west and I can see no end to the shaping of the gun. It gets ever easier to use, the skill gone. The father does not need to show the son how, and intelligence and reasoning has gone from the art of loading a gun, which once took patience and practice. Now drunks believe themselves badmen and shootists.

I get my hair cut and even the barber holds a Colt at his coin box. I tell him that nearly forty years ago I was selling those guns, that I was the first to hold them. He brushes the hair from my collar and raises his eyes. He is half my age. To them the revolver is theirs not mine.

I think of Henry Adams's letters that we see now and then in the *New York Times* and the contention that the war past was won only by the science of the repeating gun. As Meriwether Lewis had extolled the infinity of the wind-rifle, so Adams could see the future. As I could. As I had.

The engines he will have invented will be beyond his strength to control. Someday science may have the

227

existence of mankind in its power, and the human
race commit suicide, by blowing up the world.

I still dream of that circus tent from time to time. There is the man in the red coat, tall hat, and greasepaint, and sometimes his red coat is cut crudely at the back and there are giggles from the dark that I do not like.

There is a malevolence that seeps toward me, figures cut out from the white lamp. I try to wish them gone and try to fight them gone but my hands are small and I cannot go against them or against the crowd that presses to drown me. There are men in black coats and high collars and I can smell iron and sulfur all around.

But he appears then. Always.

He is in a darker black than them, darker than them counterfeits could ever pretend to be. He has renounced age. The blade of his pistol's sight has not dimmed in his eye.

He is the dry lightning that stirred me to dreaming. And they retreat.

They go back into the dark. Away from the actual. And I go back to sleep.

ACKNOWLEDGMENTS

My thanks to my agent, James Gill, ever stalwart. Katie Espiner at HarperCollins for taking it on. Thanks to Thomas McNulty, author, who kindly read my early drafts with no reason to do so and made me feel I was on the right track.

And I owe a great debt to the historical chroniclers of 19th century America whose diaries, studies and dictionaries helped me travel the road.

A CONVERSATION WITH
ROBERT LAUTNER

It's hard to believe this is the first novel about the Paterson, a gun that has played such a powerful role in the history of the United States and its culture— were you surprised when you found out there was no other such literature out there? How did you come across the story of Colt's first invention?

I couldn't believe that no-one had written about it before. To put it in perspective we had gone hundreds of years with single shot weapons and if you include cannon we're talking almost half a millennium. The only alternative was multiple barreled guns or the air-gun and its kind as mentioned in the story. This was mostly due to the unreliability of early gunpowder and the possibility that if a gun carried several charges they might all 'chain-fire' that is go off all at once and possibly maim or kill the bearer. The invention of fulminate powder and the percussion cap led directly to the possibility of a reliable repeating firearm. Colt's invention was a turning point and brought us into a new age. My coming to the story was purely from a childhood fascination of guns. I always knew the legend of Colt carving the parts of his first gun out of a ship's wooden block when he was still a teenager aboard a clipper ship and I loved the idea of this deadly weapon made only out of wood. The idea was that it is just the shape of a gun that can instil fear. The first scene that came to me, and which the whole book centered around, was what type of man could walk into a room filled with armed murderers with only a wooden gun. It was that question and getting to that scene that drove the engine of the book.

In the book something occurs which at first read is

just part of the narrative but I hope it goes deeper than that. One of the elements of the story is the introduction of the first true repeating weapon, the first practical revolver both in terms of manufacture and ability. The climactic scene with Henry Stands and Thomas Heywood's gang in the bar outside of Stroud is the *first* gunfight in history. I didn't point it out in the narrative as I didn't want to force it or break up the drama of the scene but I hope readers and observers pick up on it.

Before this point in history the pistol was a finishing weapon, after the rifle shot, for trappers and hunters, or tools for sailors and soldiers, or masterpieces for princes. Gentlemen dueled with single-shot weapons, and bad men did the same, often having to carry more than one firearm if faced with more enemies. Here we have a fight in a saloon where for the first time one man with one gun could dispatch five, and as that clearly wasn't enough we quickly moved to six shots in the hand, and then more with each generation.

With Heywood and his gang and Henry Stands we see a scene where the combatants together have at their disposal twenty-five shots to hail around a room. It is the future of violence, a different world. From that point on the evolution of the gun is the evolution of man's downfall against his brother. Imagine a world where we still had single shot weapons. Wars would probably not need fewer young men and no fewer of them would die but we might not have the day-to-day violence and murder that we abhor but expect in the civilian world and accept as inevitable. With the repeating and then automatic weapon and full-metal jacket projectile the patience and skill of loading and firing a gun became consigned to history; children can do it, and have, and we read about the consequences with heartbreak. Thomas Walker stands on a pivot of history. He witnesses the first gunfight and so do you.

THE ROAD TO RECKONING is so rich with historical detail; how do you balance the requirements of research with telling a compelling story? Do you start with the history, or the story? How do they inform each other in your writing process?

I start with the story. In fact I've noticed that I usually start with an object and ask myself, 'How did this get here?' I think most historical novelists would rather spend all their time doing research; you just get lost in it sometimes and go off in wonderful tangents. The trick is to research as you go. Get the story out as quickly as possible because that's the burning thing and you mustn't let it go out, then go back and start again with everything you've learned on the way and fill in the blanks. You'll find that what you've learned will manipulate the story to new levels that you couldn't have known of at the start. It's organic writing over formulaic.

In your writing, do you plan the story out before you begin writing, or do you start writing without an end in mind? Was there anything that surprised you in your writing of THE ROAD TO RECKONING, which you didn't expect to happen?

I always have a rough idea of the path of the story written down. This is usually stages that I want to get to, scenes I've imagined, and between these blocks of scenes is the story. I can't say that I always have an ending in mind. As I fill in the blocks they mutate, sometimes vanish and new ones come and the story does what it wants to do. In my opinion if you plot out a novel entirely you won't be able to surprise yourself or your reader. I feel that plotting a book completely is a very old-fashioned style of story-telling. Readers are more sophisticated now. I don't mean they're more intelligent it's just that we see so much more television and movies than readers before us that we can spot plots, endings and story arcs faster than audiences used to and if I don't know how my story ends than it's impossible for my reader to do the same. I hate reading a book when I know exactly how it ends by chapter three. I believe books are our last indulgence. If you're willing to spend so much time with me I'll do what I can to reward that indulgence.

I was surprised by the cannibal Strother Gore. He came from a dream. I had become fascinated by the stories of the mines in my research and the sadness of all these abandoned towns and I came across a lot of cannibal stories from settlers and foresters. I imagined this kind of Gollum-like creature still holding out, as abandoned as the mines and towns. His appearance is what I like to call a 'hurricane moment.' It's usually at the point in the book where the reader is totally settled, thinks he knows where it's going and then 'BAM! You didn't see that coming did you?' Strother was that moment. I felt I needed to give Thomas another jeopardy, something timeless, something outside the fear of getting killed and something that a young person or anyone so used to zombies and monsters that are no longer monsters, could still fear. And cannibals are almost of the old world of horror, something that should be supernatural, demonic but is still very much of the real world. The horror is that we all know that something like that is happening right now and we'll read about it only when they get caught or never read about it because they never get caught. I didn't want a child killer or a molester; that's an easy card that so many writers use. I don't believe in shock and gore as entertainment unless it's for that particular audience. Strother doesn't care that Thomas is a child and that was my intention. I hoped that that scene would bring the reader back to the childhood fear of losing your parents, of being alone and then someone comes for you, and not someone good, but the hope is that your father will always find you and he'll be bigger and stronger than the bad man.

All of the story's characters are powerfully memorable, but Henry Stands in particular stands out as someone who's impossible to forget. Is Henry based on a real historical figure? Did any of the other characters have historical precedents?

I based Henry on an amalgam of people and characters. Historically it was General Tecumseh Sherman and Wyatt Earp. I had pictures of Sherman around me all the time and read his memoirs throughout writing the book, and have you ever seen a picture of Earp when he was an old man? That's Henry's face.

There's also a book called *The Story of the Outlaw* by Emerson Hough printed in 1907 which is a serious study of desperadoes of the west in the 19th century. Some of the characters in that study became Henry Stands and Thomas Heywood and his gang. Other inspirations are a mix of movie actors I grew up with. The older Wayne and Eastwood, and especially Lee Marvin, are all there.

The hotel owner, Mrs Hollinshead, Judge Stokes and the mail carrier, Dean, although only briefly appear, are all real people from the history of Stroudsberg.

How did you get the idea to have Thomas named after the Washington Irving character? What significance does that have for you?

That's a component that I use in my writing. It may be a character's name or a painting or book mentioned in the story and the idea is that the reader goes and has a look at that and then gets another understanding about the character or the book's other characters and themes. I think it's a development of the 'show, don't tell' rule. I don't have to 'tell' at all! In this instance it refers to the fact that the hard times we have now have always been and always will be as long as greed is a motive and speculation designed to benefit the few and break the rest. And the Devil has his hand in it.

One of the most powerful themes of the story is the relationship between fathers and sons. Do you have

sons who have read the book? Has your father read it? How did your own past inspire your perspective on the nature of the father-son bond?

One of my reasons for writing the book was so that my sons could read it. I have four sons, ranging in age from two to twenty-two and I wanted to write something that they could all read at some point. Fathers and sons have issues. They have a bond but it's seldom expressed and I don't see any harm in that. It should be father first and friend second. Where I bond is in toys and movies. My father is old-school Catholic-Irish so unless it's about horses or Irish history he doesn't read! My own present perhaps has more to do with the story than my past. When I had my third son I realized I was at the age my father was when he had me and you always see your father as older but suddenly he became a young man to me. I realized he probably had the same doubts and problems and sacrificed his own pursuits for his children as I do. You always see your parents as assured and confident if you're lucky enough, but from then on I saw him as an older me and not just my dad.

The novel takes place at such an interesting time in American history, when the exploration of the west was really beginning in earnest. What interests you about that particular era? How do you see the role of the Colt in the exploration of the west?

My interest in the era was that I wanted to show another time when the country was in depression, on the cusp of industrialization, going from horse to steam, canal to rail and entering into a new age of firearms. I wanted to show how with regards to economics nothing has changed. This is an ongoing thing. It will always be. It's an economic constant. It's how economics works. People think that the whole 'one-percent' thing is a product of modern times. It's as old as civilization. It's only subtle in the story but the idea is one of hope. Thomas's father is taking a risk on a new venture. He's taking a chance. He's holding the future in his hands, maybe a bad future, maybe something that will just improve war but merit sometimes springs from wars and we advance. It's not governments that move us on; governments just want everything to stay the same. Individuals change things. Colt's guns changed America. What they gave to the settlers was an easy to use weapon to defend their homes and gave the army firepower to settle those lands. The expansion of America is directly related to the improvement of the gun and transportation. The limits of the canals was removed by the railroad and the limits of offense and defense expanded by the development of the metal jacketed round and the repeating firearm. Both became uglier. Progress is not pretty. Another reason for choosing Thomas Walker's name was the development of the Colt Walker. I didn't want that to be a coincidence. It was the most powerful handgun in the world for almost a hundred years. Our phones get upgraded every six months. That weapon was a pinnacle of achievement in its field for nearly a hundred years.

What can we expect from you next? Would you ever consider working with any of the characters from THE ROAD TO RECKONING again?

I have considered working with the characters again. Obviously Henry Stands is still alive and I am intrigued by the Fellenberg idea of institutional schooling as mentioned in the novel. What would it be like to go that school? And Thomas is an adult now. He'd be good for another story!

Listen to Robert Lautner talk about *The Road to Reckoning* on the BookD Podcast.

Subscribe on iTunes or find it on
Souncloud: https://soundcloud.com/bookdpodcast/
robert-lautner-and-murder